DREAM TALES

AND OTHER
SHORT STORIES

I0663289

ELSA WOLF

Copyright ©2025 by Elsa Wolf
elsawolfbooks
elsawolf@yahoo.com
Interior design and cover by Champagne Book Design

Library of Congress Control Number: 2025915685
Wolf, Elsa
Dream Tales, And Other Short Stories / 1st ed.
ISBN 978-1-7327774-5-3 (pbk)
ISBN 978-1-7327774-6-0 (ebook)
ISBN 978-7327774-7-7 (hrdbk)

Laramie, Wyoming
United States of America

ALSO BY ELSA WOLF

Buried Truths, A Daughter's Tale...
Adoption and discovery with an international flare

Keep Me Forever...
A novel about a young man's struggles with decisions, romance,
and PTSD

Available in paperback and eBook

There is a psychological technique which makes it possible to interpret dreams, and … if that procedure is employed, every dream reveals itself as a psychical structure which has a meaning and which can be inserted at an assigned point in the mental activities of the waking life.

—Sigmund Freud

Falling asleep while reading a book. Dreaming you are one of the characters. Choose your books wisely.

—Unknown

AUTHOR'S NOTE

There are three parts in this collection of short stories. The first rose from the depths of my dreams, those strange and vivid hours when the mind roams untethered. The second holds mysteries born of places I've wandered—two cases, two countries, one detective who never stops until the last secret falls. The third is a meeting ground—some stories walk alone, others thread their way back to my first novel, *Buried Truths, A Daughter's Tale.* Each story was written with the hope that you'd feel the same pull that first drew me to this journey.

CONTENTS

DREAM TALES

AND OTHER
SHORT STORIES

WHAT A DREAM I HAD

Oh, my—
what a dream I had,
when I stood by the edge of the sea,
and the mighty surf rolled in,
steady and sure,
like breath.
I walked on soft, sweet pine needles
beneath ancient, whispering trees
their voices older than memory,
gentler than time.
I slipped into a book,
or let the music carry me—
a thread of melody,
a sigh in the dark.
I talked for hours into the night
With this one,
Or that—
As if the stars had nowhere to be.
Oh, my—
what a dream I had
Of love,
And work,
And ideas.

—Gretchen Wolf

PART ONE

DREAMS

THE ECHO WAREHOUSE

"Hold d'it in… Hold d'it in…" A surge of anxiety gripped Luna's chest. She tried to soothe herself, murmuring under her breath, "Don't cry again! Not now!" She lightly slapped her own cheek for talking out loud to no one in particular, while wishing she had more than her own company. Cities always made her uneasy, but there was nowhere else to go. Luna had loaded her worldly possessions into her dad's ancient Buick sedan and driven away from the mountains with her antiquated map. Her soul felt hollow without her husband by her side. They didn't have any children, and their parents were long gone. Losing Will and his crew in the factory accident was almost too much to bear. There was no one left and nothing to do but move forward, one step at a time, into an uncertain future.

The scant reparations she'd received from the factory were gone, and the money she received from the family trust fund was barely enough to sustain her. Forms could be filled out to increase her distribution, but she hadn't found the emotional energy to tackle the bureaucratic maze. The promise of a new job offered her hope in the midst of her internal darkness. After she was settled in this city, she'd deal with the paperwork. There wasn't much choice in the matter; the cost of an apartment would be exorbitant, and every penny saved counted. Luna had heard a studio apartment with eighty-square-feet could be over a thousand dollars a month. The resurfacing of this thought alone would make anyone's eyes water.

Ten years ago, Luna had turned her back on her family and her corporate career to join her husband in upstate New York. There,

1

he'd worked in a factory creating furniture. Her parents disapproved of the life she'd chosen with Will—a small cabin nestled in the woods far from the nearest neighbors. But they liked him well enough, even loved him. They had wanted more for their daughter, yet she was sure they didn't wish him dead.

Lost among the unfamiliar streets of New York City, she wove through a maze of one-way streets, around orange barriers and spilled containers of garbage that threatened her quest for a new beginning. The debris seemed to mock her, a reminder of the fragility of human existence. She swerved to avoid the debris and the excessive number of pigeons flitting amongst the piles. A stuffed bear, a Christmas gift from Will, tumbles off a pile of boxes in the backseat. She picked him up and kissed his nose. Overhead, crows swooped back and forth. Distracted by the mayhem, she barely avoided a cat racing across the street after an oversized rodent.

The stench of the city's rancid aroma assaulted her senses. The heat of the day magnified the odor. She rolled up the window in an unsuccessful attempt to escape the noxious fumes, but they seeped through every crevice, clinging to her like a shroud. It was simply too quiet in New York City. Where was everyone? There should be cars, buses, taxis, and pedestrians all around since the electricity crisis was over. Feeling rather conspicuous despite the absence of people or vehicles on the road, Luna wished she had a more modern car.

Then she realized, other than the pigeons and crows, she hadn't seen or heard any melodic birds. The countryside where she had lived before was filled with the gentle chirping of cardinals, sparrows, finches, herons, and bluebirds.

Turning on the radio, Luna learned why no one was moving through the city. All the businesses were closed until mid-week, even though the power was back on. The fallout from the previous weeklong outage had brought the city to its knees. Food had gone rancid, communication had failed when computer batteries ran low, and air-conditioning systems were useless without back-up generators.

Several deaths were reported as a result of poorly installed generators leaking fumes into enclosed areas. The broadcaster's voice faded. She thought back to her childhood when a family in her school had left a generator running all night in a garage. The fumes trickled into the house and asphyxiated the occupants. A lesson learned, and not easily forgotten by any adult, much less a child. Back then, there wasn't any counseling for children or their families to learn how to cope with loss. A memorial was held. Afterwards, everyone was expected to go on with life as usual, as if the lost family had never existed. This wasn't easy, especially for the school friends of deceased peers. Luna knew them well and often cried herself to sleep at night while her mother banged pots around in the kitchen sink.

Focusing back on the broadcaster, he droned on about the history of the older buildings in New York. People with windows that opened were the only winners, as the air became stale in the newer ones with fixed, sealed windows. This was especially true on sweltering days when the humidity and temperature were above eighty degrees. For unknown reasons, architects deemed this decision a good economic one to prevent HVAC systems from overloading if anyone left a window open indefinitely. With the electricity off for days, none of the economics mattered to anyone stuck in those situations. So, no one functioned after dark without flashlights or candles. Many people chose to hunker down in bed when the sun slept rather than fight with battery operated lights or dripping candle wax and the potential fires that could occur if they fell asleep without extinguishing the flame. The radio commentary only depressed Luna more. She wondered why she had to move to such a place after the tranquility of living in the countryside with fields of green grass and hundreds of trees in the surrounding woodlands.

When she reached the intersection closest to her final destination on the one-way street in Manhattan, she parked in the first available curbside spot near an alleyway. A sense of relief washed over her. The journey had been long and arduous, but she had finally arrived. Yet, as she tried to step out of the car with her crossover purse, she realized she'd parked too close to an eight-foot, or was it a ten-foot, light post. The door opened about six inches. She put a leg out and pulled herself up, using the top of the door to no avail. Cursing her own carelessness, she wished she was still rail thin. Thudding back onto the seat, she realized she'd parked on the wrong side of the street and had gone down the one-way road in the wrong direction. The driver's door needed to face the center of the road. With no other cars in sight, she U-turned on the road to rectify her error. The last time she'd made such a mistake, she'd been in a rental car in England, where everyone drove on the left side of the road. *God, it was a lifetime ago. Maybe fifteen years had passed since then.*

Getting out this time with her purse was easier, but the passenger door remained obstructed next to another light post. She'd figure out how to remove her belongings after finding the job-site. Staring up toward the halogen light, she noticed every available inch on the post had been covered with cards and posters. One said; *all is well.* She very much doubted that. Another sign stated that cars could park for a maximum of two hours after payment. But where was the machine? She'd used these units before and knew it would ask for her license plate number. Pulling out her cellphone, she moved around to the back of the car and snapped a picture. Whenever she was anxious, numbers dropped out of her mind. She walked down to the nearest corner, looking for the payment machine without finding it. Turning around, she rushed past her car and found it a half block away. As she pushed buttons, she became annoyed. It didn't operate the same way she remembered. What if the power had glitched the system and she couldn't pay? There were four different ways to use her credit card: slide the bar code, insert the chip, tap the scanner, or use an app on a phone. The scanner looked sun-bleached. The slide bar had a piece of chewing gum stuck in it. It took several tries before the chip registered. The idea of beating the machine came to mind. The days of using real coins were so much easier, but finding some in the depths of her car would create another challenge. Everything that should be easy wasn't these days. Too many choices. The simplest task often brought tears of frustration to her eyes.

Back by the car, to safeguard herself from prowling meter maids, she affixed a note to the dashboard with her phone number to circumvent any trouble. The allotted two hours should be plenty of time to meet her employer and find a permanent parking solution. Stuffing her phone back in her purse, she pulled out her employment letter and found the address. She hurried along Fifth Avenue in search of the building. When she arrived, the structure was much taller and narrower than any she'd ever seen before. The towering monolith almost vanished between the surrounding wider structures. Reaching out to touch the door, she expected it to be hot, but the textured stainless-steel material was cold. When she pressed a button on the communicator unit, a surge of anticipation fluttered in her chest. Waiting, waiting. No one responded.

Luna pushed on the door. At first, it was unyielding, but then it released and swung open against the adjacent wall. Her excitement gave way to confusion. The space before her stretched out endlessly, a vast warehouse filled with shadows. With renewed anxiety and hesitation, her eyes scanned the dimly lit interior for any sign of life. Stepping inside, she observed dust particles floating through streams of light coming from elongated windows fifteen feet or so above her head up by a metal, beamed ceiling. The light highlighted some areas and left others in total darkness. Luna blinked, her mind struggling to comprehend while her eyes adjusted to her new surroundings.

"Hello? Is anyone here?" Luna called out, her voice echoing in the cavernous space.

"Yes, come closer." A melodic falsetto voice replied in the darkness. A moment later, a woman stepped into the beams of sunlight. Her long wavy dark hair piled askew on top of her head in a tangled mess. She appeared larger across the middle than her gaunt extremities implied, likely because of the quantity of ragged, multi-colored fabric coiled around her like a snake. Every inch of the woman's face had been overtaken by wrinkles.

"Hello." Luna shivered, crossed her arms over her waist and then released them. She didn't want to appear unappreciative or scared, but she was. The woman reminded her of the wicked witch in the old German fairy tale, *Hansel and Gretel*. "Um, this building isn't quite what I expected. I'm supposed to start work in clothing distribution. The man who interviewed me—Mr. Snit—didn't tell me much. He just said I should come and find a woman."

"That's my name. Sorry, I wasn't in the video interview, but I don't like modern gadgets." She raised her arms, and the overhead lights came on.

Instead of commenting on the rows of tables with clothing piled high, Luna said, "Woman?"

"I am one, so as I said, that's my name." Without further explanation, Woman grabbed a pile of cloth topped with brass jewelry and handed it to Luna with spools of thread.

Luna pressed her chin into the pile, and her voice came out muffled. "What?"

"Organize them into categories and put them in the wicker baskets under the tables. Don't be overwhelmed by the quantity. All the items are donated. The newer ones should be sold. I use the rest for my projects. You're in charge of the entire sorting and sales process. Computers are the bane of my existence, so I can't manage this aspect of the business."

"Right. Yes, ma'am." Luna was too overwhelmed to object to the order. Her stomach lurched. She guessed the warehouse might have been a sweatshop where many women had worked long, hard hours more than a hundred years ago. This place was nothing like the corporate offices she'd been in years before.

"I have urgent business elsewhere at a hospice facility. Time is of the essence. Transfers to load." Woman grabbed a rack of empty glass vials off a shelf. "I keep the full ones in a refrigeration unit in another room. Please don't touch anything in there." She turned away, opened the door, and a searing light flooded the room. A second later, Woman vanished along with the light.

"I don't understand," Luna mumbled to herself. The colored cloth still hung across her arms. She moved forward to an empty table and let the items tumble onto the surface. Spreading everything out, she realized they were pieces of clothing. Before getting to work, she took time to look around.

Massive mounds of garments standing at least six-feet tall formed the shape of upside-down ice cream cones on the tables. In the background, between the tables, there was a closed door.

A voice spoke from behind her. "Hello, I'm Finn."

She spun around, startled. Realizing it was probably another worker, she paused and extended her hand. "I'm Luna."

"My hands are covered in oil, can't shake, sorry." The dark-skinned man smiled. His brilliant teeth glistened in the dim light.

"Woman said something about transfers." Luna frowned. "What was she talking about?"

"It's not my place to explain." Finn stared at Luna. "I can tell you the refrigeration room has floor to ceiling shelves of vials. They are all labeled and dated. Women will explain the rest. She has been at this task for a hundred years. Or so she says. Don't mention I told you anything."

"Yes, all right." Not knowing what else to do, Luna asked for directions to the bathroom before excusing herself. As she secured the door, she took out her cell phone from the pocket of her overalls and called Mr. Snit, using the automatic redial function. He didn't answer. After some meditative deep breaths, Luna unlocked the door and wandered through the building.

Opening one of the closed doors, she saw thirteen dark wooden desks. Six school desks lined one side of the room and six on the other. In each student chair sat a stiff figure with a hand holding a pencil over a pile of paper, as if waiting to record the teacher's words. At the head of the class sat a massive desk with another figure standing behind it in front of a blackboard.

"Excuse me?" Luna feebly inquired.

None of the figures moved or said a word.

"They're not alive, yet." A voice echoed behind her.

She looked over her shoulder. "Oh, Finn, you startled me. I'm not sure what to make of this place. What are these things? These people?" She left the room without closing the door.

Finn followed and said, "They're life-size dolls of a sort—androids."

"I didn't know this could be done. It's unnerving."

"This isn't the only room. There are others with different themes. People pay for this. For being transferred. Crap, I wasn't supposed to explain. Woman's idea is to have employees get used to the place before explanations are given."

"Okay." She drew out the word. "I won't mention it to her. But this is all unnatural or immoral or something beyond my understanding."

"I felt the same way when I first arrived. If you need the job, you'll get used to it. Aren't their eyes incredible?"

"I guess," Luna replied. Returning to the main room, she walked farther down the aisle. She looked to the left side of the aisle to what appeared to be females in skirts or dresses. On the right, there were only boys in slacks and shirts with ties. Directing her attention back to the girl next to her, Luna gazed into her eyes. They weren't glass, but a solidified jelly with vivid hazel irises. The skin appeared to be a tinted polymer with a flawless complexion. The eyebrows were thin brown lines, followed up by a full head of auburn hair flowing down the back of her outfit. The fingers were long and lean, with every joint creased and authentically painted to perfection. But then, without warning, the hand holding the pen moved across the page.

Luna jumped back a few steps. She moved closer and examined the writing. It was the letter 'D' with stylized curves.

"Gave you quite a start." Finn's nose wrinkled into a laugh. "There are other rooms with different scenes besides the schoolroom."

"I never expected this place. It's weird. Maybe I should have asked more questions, but I'm almost out of money, and this is the only job I could find. I stopped searching after I'd sent out thirty-plus resumes."

"You'll get used to it. The rooms in the loft are okay. One of them has your name etched on a piece of wood on the floor. It's a gloomy area. No windows. If you're nervous, lock up at night."

"I want to get an apartment in the city at some point."

"Be careful with what you pick. The history of lodgings is pretty sketchy. You'll find a lot of undesirable places." Finn ran his hand through his curly mop of black hair.

"Like?"

"Like some of them don't have enough air circulation. Back in the 1800s, buildings were put up pretty quick to house immigrant workers. The bosses didn't want to spend a lot of money, which is ironic since apartments and homes are crazy expensive now."

"Did they get fixed up in the last two-hundred years?" Luna asked, chuckling under her breath.

"When tuberculous hit hard, the bosses put windows in the hall doors for cross ventilation in some buildings and ventilation shafts in others. Then there was the Spanish flu, which wiped out even more people."

"Don't forget COVID-19."

"How could I. Lost my mom to that beast."

"I'm sorry."

"Thanks. There was nothing I could do. She died alone in the hospital. I wasn't allowed to visit the quarantine ward." He paused. "Back to what I was saying. There's this one building where the vent shaft became a trash chute. The story goes—a woman lost her husband to one of those diseases and threw herself down the shaft, hoping to die, but the trash softened her landing. She survived."

"I'm sure I didn't want to know the details. I bet there are ghosts everywhere in those places. Hopefully, I can find a modern apartment without those types of glitches."

"Perhaps." Finn strolled across the room into a corridor kitchen. He pulled two containers of food out of a metal cabinet resembling an old-fashioned vending machine. Luna followed him with her eyes and then felt as if magnets were pulling her into the room behind him.

Pointing, he continued, "This refrigerated slot is yours. It gets stocked each day, but I don't know who does the honors. I'm not sure how it actually stays cool without a door. One of Woman's magic tricks, I suppose. Reminds me of a *Star Trek* food replicator. Big fan of the show."

"I've seen a few of those. And thanks, I'm pretty hungry." She interrupted, took the container, and began eating. With her mouth full, she said, "I've got a lot of sorting to do. Where's your workstation?" Luna thought the guy seemed normal compared to everything else.

"Through that door." Finn gestured across the room. "I lube and maintain the machines that make the dolls. No one other than me and the artist—I call him that, but I think he's more of a scientist—can go in there without Woman's permission. Don't know why, it's just her way. She'll be back soon with new transfers. Don't know how she does the transfer. She kicks us out of the room."

"There's a lot you don't seem to know."

"That's the way," Finn said.

"Okay. So, another subject." Luna read the time on her phone. "My car is in a two-hour slot on the street. Where can I move it for permanent parking?"

"Back of the building. Go half way round the block. You'll see a tucked in area with a dumpster and four parking spots. My electric hybrid car's there, plugged into a port. It's gray with tinted windows."

"Mine's not electric."

"You're missing out. They're great."

"Doesn't seem like it. If the power outages continue, I think I've got the better deal."

"True, but this is the first one I've seen. Maybe we'll get lucky and there won't be anymore." He chuckled. "Park your car next to the dumpster. We need to get back to our assignment before Woman returns. If we're slackers, she won't pay us. Work a solid hour and a half before you move your car."

Luna went over to the sorting tables without delay. She wondered what this place, with so little light, held beyond Finn's doors. Not liking her dark thoughts and growing paranoia, she put a garment in its matching color pile, then hesitated, reconsidered and subdivided them by size, then sex, then age. Two baskets became four, then eight, and on and on.

After an hour passed, she heard a noise. It came from the classroom; the head desk chair was empty. The occupant stood at a blackboard writing. Luna walked a little closer and noticed another figure across the room in the shadows. The letters on the board curved up and down in lines across the surface. The first formed a string of words written in a neon yellow chalk —*not what I expected this would be. I'm Professor Brandice.* Under that, the professor began writing mathematical computations. A voice came from somewhere deep inside as she recited the process. Then Luna understood. This android had been a teacher before her soul traveled out of her body at death, was captured in one of Woman's storage vials, and deposited back into the thing. Luna shuddered to think about the possibility of her deceased husband being trapped inside one and was grateful she hadn't known about this type of life extension.

HAIR ON THE ROAD

The streets of D.C. were eerily deserted during Blake's Sunday morning walk with her cocker spaniel. The city's iconic landmarks, such as the White House and the National Archives, held their enigmatic secrets, along with the FBI and the countless government buildings. Blake thought about those places often, as she'd worked in some of them as an administrative assistant over the last decade. Today, none of that held any significance other than to mull over her accomplishments while she strolled along with her dog, Jiffy, who had been named after her favorite peanut butter. He began pulling her away from their daily course along the tranquil sidewalk onto the street. At first, Blake resisted, but then trusted the unspoken bond between them. Even so, she cautiously scanned the street for unexpected vehicles while moving forward. Jiffy led the way and stopped at a wig-like clump of black hair, which appeared to be crowning on the edge of the asphalt road. Blake's imagination briefly toyed with the idea of a hidden sinkhole. The theory dropped out of her mind since they are funnel shaped with a large opening at the street level that would narrow down to the end of a pool of water. It seemed no human could be bobbing up and down in one so small. Then, much to her surprise, the hair moved ever so slightly to the left and then to the right. It looked like a baby's head emerging askew during childbirth. Yet, the protruding skullcap was the size of a full-grown adult.

Jiffy's initial growl, deep in his throat, soon gave way to a whimper. Blake continued to stare in disbelief at the site and its backdrop. The speck of motor oil, the ground-in old French fries, a wad of chewed gum, and a dollop of dried vomit. Her jaw clenched, and she suppressed a gag. A moment of panic overtook her mind, and she glanced upward at the surrounding office buildings, hoping to signal someone even if she couldn't explain why their attention was needed. The dog might be wrong. There might be no cause for alarm. Perhaps the twitching hair was nothing more than a costume wig stirred by gentle breezes. Struggling to make sense of it all, she couldn't help but recall the stories of children who had fallen into narrow wells and been stuck for days.

In a voice barely above a whisper, Blake said, "Hello? You. Down there. Is someone there?"

The voice that emerged—a squeak—sounded like an animal in peril.

"What? Try again," she urged.

"Help me." The voice that croaked out was not animal, but human. A fact beyond dispute. The hair moved down an inch or so, and two beefy fingers slid up next to the edge of the opening. The tips were bloodied, and the shafts streaked with a black, unidentifiable substance.

"Hold on. I'll call 9-1-1." For a moment, she paused. How would she explain? With a trembling hand, she pulled her phone from her front pocket and dialed. Holding the phone tightly to her ear, she listened. The response was swift.

"9-1-1. What is your emergency?"

"There's a person stuck under the road. I'm at the intersection of 13th and E Street, N.W."

"Are you in danger?"

"I don't think so."

"We'll send out a unit."

That went well, she thought. *Wait until they get here, and see what I really meant.*

While they waited, Blake and Jiffy nervously paced back and forth within a six-foot radius of the peculiar 'hair'. No one seemed to be any happier. Jiffy sat down by the 'hair' in protest, and Blake started talking about the weather or the dog's daily habits in a loop of chatter with the intent of helping the 'hair' feel more at ease. But she worried the circular chatter might have had the opposite effect, since it was making her shoulders and stomach tense. Changing her tactics, she turned on some instrumental music on her phone to soothe all concerned. The necessity to jockey around ended when an ambulance appeared with a firetruck and a police car close behind.

A police officer approached and identified himself. "Hello, I'm Captain Kane. What's the problem?"

She pointed at the person's head. "Hey, you down there. I got help. Show your fingers again and say something."

The person followed her instructions.

"What the hell?" Captain Kane removed his cap and rubbed his head in solidarity. "Ma'am, please take your dog and sit back on the sidewalk. We may need to talk to you again." He turned away. "Excuse me."

Blake complied with his request and listened intently from the sidelines. None of her friends were going to believe this story. It might even end up in the local news. She watched the sergeant lumber toward the ambulance and then the fire truck. Upon his return with a fireman at his heals, she noticed a cellphone in a transparent case with a lanyard attached to his belt along with one without a case in his shirt pocket. Over by the vehicles, the remaining emergency responders were hovering in a circle. She presumed they were strategizing or waiting for follow-up instructions.

Addressing the person below once more, Captain Kane said, "So, person down there. I'm a police officer. I'm here with an ambulance and a fire truck. Can you lower your head? I want to send in a videophone to figure out how to help."

The hair descended, allowing the phone to be lowered.

"Look at that... a window to underground tunnels..." Captain Kane asked. "Hey, how'd you get in there?"

The victim's rough voice floated forth, but Blake couldn't tell what was said. The conversation continued with the captain.

"A mudlarker? What's that?" He said with a bewildered expression. "Never mind. We'll get you out. Hold on."

⚬

Over by the fire engine, the two paramedics sat idly by while the police officer and the fire crew huddled together, expressing their uncertainty about the situation. The police officer began to engage the others. "You ever seen anything like this?"

"No, what an ass," said fireman number one.

Amidst the deliberation, paramedic one said, "What are we going to do?"

"How the F#@$%! do we get in there?" said a junior firefighter.

"Let's just leave him there," said another fireman with a sneer. "We'll have to dig up the road with a backhoe. It'll take hours to even get one."

"Seriously? The victim will be dehydrated and hungry by then." Paramedic two said.

"There has to be a manhole nearby." The junior fireman said while rubbing his chin.

"I'll go have a look," said Captain Kane.

"While you're at it, I'll check the city's underground maps." The junior firefighter said and began scrolling through his iPad. "Here we go. It's called the D.C. Water Atlas. No, not helpful. Hang on… found it. The Army Corps of Engineers' plans are more complete." Turning the iPad towards the group, he showed them the path.

After a substantial amount of bantering among the team, Captain Kane returned, indicating he had found a manhole fifty-feet down the road. The paramedics pulled out a gurney from the ambulance and a medical supply bag, along with a collapsible stretcher to take down into the hole in case they had to carry the victim out. The paramedics scurried along the road, with the junior firefighter following behind with a crowbar. The junior fire-fighter would be the lucky one who'd have to go in first with his headlamp ablaze.

The junior firefighter pushed the crowbar into a slot in the manhole. Pulling it up was more challenging for his pumped bi-ceps than expected. While he struggled and ratcheted the lid, a visible shiver passed across his shoulders. Popping it off, he tossed the cover and the crowbar to the side. Below him, the black claus-trophobic hole stared back. His training hadn't quite prepared him for going into such a place. Another firefighter ran over and handed the three men yellow construction helmets and tossed the junior firefighter a hand-held radio to clip onto his belt. With an audible click of the switches, they all turned on their helmet lights. One of the paramedics distributed masks to protect them from potential pathogens.

The junior firefighter descended into the darkness with the headlamp providing a narrow beam of clarity. The two paramed-ics went in next, swiftly carrying the folded stretcher with balleri-na-like balance.

At the bottom, the junior firefighter patted his pocket to con-firm he had his cellphone just in case the radio communications with the surface failed or if they needed additional assistance with the route. Scanning the area with the torches, the light confirmed that the walls of the culvert were old. According to the rapid re-search topside, the system started its meandering around D.C. in the late 1800s. The tunnels' brick walls were speckled with a mys-terious black, mold-like substance. Below them flowed a narrow subterranean brook flanked by pipes. The air was hazy and car-ried a modicum of an underlying aroma similar to a moss filled terrarium.

Walking along the raised sides of the waterway was a bit of a balancing act due to its twelve-inch width and uneven surface. At several spots along the passageway, one of their boots slipped into the water and stirred up silt or aggravated a black water snake. The junior firefighter's light flashed into a deeper area of the water, and he froze mid-breath. He imagined a pair of eyes peering up at him.

The distance to the victim wasn't long in paces, but being in the darkness made it feel like it was double the expected length. When they arrived next to the man, he was crouching on a ledge, shivering. They wrapped him in a blanket and assessed his condition while he warmed up. The stretcher they'd slogged in with them wasn't needed. Once the 'hair' was accompanied by lights and guides, he walked on his own back to the ladder and ascended through the manhole into the sunlight wrapped in a smudged blanket, clutching a container the size of a child's shoe box. Up on the street, a paramedic exchanged the dirty blanket for a clean one and draped it over his shoulder while he positioned himself on the gurney.

"Miss, he wants to talk to you." The paramedic called out. She stood up. Jiffy strained on the leash. Within seconds, they were right next to the gurney.

"Hello? It looks like you're okay," Blake said.

"Thank you. Name's Charles."

"I'm Blake. Are you related to Prince Charles?" She was trying to lighten the mood with a joke. He looked nothing like royalty, with his curly hair matted to his head and his clothes smeared with dirt.

"No, love." His words came out scratchy. To recover, he grabbed a water bottle off the gurney's pillow and drank it down. He might have been around her age. Maybe a little older than thirty, but it was hard to tell with the scratches on his face. The paramedics disinfected the marks while wiping off the rest of his visible complexion and determined no further action on their part was required. A long soak in a hot bathtub and a change of clothes would do him a world of good.

"Sorry we had to meet like this." Charles cleared his throat and offered a warm, albeit somewhat strained, smile, with his puppy dog eyes.

"Well, nice to meet you, Charles." Blake couldn't think of anything else to start with while eyeing a dirty piece of paper resting next to him on the gurney. "What's that?"

"A city permit, to snoop around the tunnels. The only stipulation was that I did it in the wee hours of the morning before the city was awake. Don't know why. No one said, and I didn't ask. Then the park service lent me a key to Ford's theater. My anthropology credentials were a big help in persuading all concerned."

After contemplating the overall situation, she said, "What's mudlarking and how did you end up here?"

"It's treasure hunting, of sorts. I learned about it in England on the Thames. There, people wait until low-tide and then muck around in the mud with gloves, looking for old relics." He paused and looked into her eyes. "I have a fascination with President Lincoln. I began my US tour out in Springfield, Illinois, at the home he lived in before becoming president. While I was there, I met a chap who told me about this guy in D.C. who dug tunnels under Dupont Circle. He was traveling between his two wives' homes incognito in the early 1900s. Named Dyar. An entomologist. This city started to sound interesting in more ways than government politics. Humans love to dig. Initially, the residents thought the tunnel was created by Union Soldiers during the Civil War. So, I started at the Ford's Theater."

"I see. No. I don't get the fascination."

"There's no monetary value involved for most mudlarkers…"

"A what?"

He scowled and explained again. "People who dig in the mud looking for things. It's relaxing and usually just a bit fun."

"Not this time," piped in the paramedic while eyeing the smudged metal box clutched in Charles's crossed arms. "You got off lucky."

"If my phone hadn't stopped working, I would have been fine." His accent was clearer now and most definitely British. "It's dark down there. I tried to retrace my steps back to where I started. I'd gone into the theater's basement and found a doorway that led into the tunnel's antechamber, and started searching for trinkets."

"That's gross," Blake said.

"Not really. It's all rainwater runoff in this area. No human sewage." Charles was quiet for a moment. "Regardless, I had better get a tetanus booster."

"Sir, what on earth was so important down there that you had to risk your life?" Captain Kane said with an edge to his voice. "You're very lucky this young lady came along."

"Yes, indeed. I'm sorry to trouble everyone. Hunting has been rather fun until now." Charles wiggled off the gurney onto his feet. The emergency crew grabbed their gear and wished him well. With shouts and clanking of equipment, they soon disappeared into their vehicles and drove away.

"Now, you're no longer pieces of hair in the road," Blake said while rolling her shoulders to release her own inner tension. "My calmer side wants to know what's in the box."

"Truly remarkable." He stroked the box, pulled up the clasp, and opened it on creaking hinges. "After what we've been through this morning, I trust you can keep my confidence."

"Sure, but you owe me," she said with a chortle.

"Fair enough." He tilted the box. In it sat a gold pocket watch, a set of bones from a human hand, and a leather bag of coins.

She gasped and brought her fingertips to her upper lip. "Oh, my, God!"

"Yes, indeed." He pointed across the street to a coffee shop and brushed off his clothes. "I'm still a bit chilled. I feel like I've been in a coal mine. Would you be interested in chatting over a cuppa? Sorry, a cup of tea or coffee?"

"Sure, why not? They shouldn't complain about the dirt on

your clothes," she said with a lopsided smile. "We can sit outside. Jiffy will settle down under the table."

They did just that. By the time their coffees and sandwiches had arrived, they'd debated on whether or not someone at the Smithsonian or the FBI should be consulted about the contents of the box. The inscription on the watch said, *To Mitch with Love— Bee.* The coins were 1886 silver dollars. If Charles wanted to know the true age of the bones, they'd have to undergo a carbon-14 analysis. Then there was the question; why were the items stored together in this fashion?

"So, other than President Lincoln being murdered at the theater, what's so special about the place? And why did you go digging around?" She took a sip of coffee. "I should know more about the place since I live here, but I've spent my time making a living instead."

"Understandable. A year after Lincoln's death in 1865, the government purchased the theater, and the Secretary of War, Edwin Stanton, converted it into an office building with an Army Medical Museum on the top floor. There's more, but I'll spare you unless you want to go tour the place during open hours?"

"Interesting stuff. I'm not sure when I can." She pushed a strand of hair behind her ear. "Go on."

"Later, in 1893, the floor collapsed, and the building was abandoned until 1932, when the National Park Service took it on and repaired the floor. In the early 1960s, the building was turned back into the original theater. I felt precious items were likely lost in the kerfuffle." He drank his coffee quickly since it was getting cold. "Let me borrow your phone." With quick motions, his fingers move back and forth. "Got it. The coins are estimated to be valued at $1,000 US. There are ten coins. Incredible!"

"It's your lucky day, if the theater doesn't claim them. Hang on." Blake stroked the edges of the watch while examining the inside of the box. A discolored green piece of felt lay under the items. "There's an edge of something." Pulling back the felt, she discovered a note folded into fourths.

To whomever finds this, it is now yours to do as you please. I should very much like to tell you what I have enclosed. To say truth, the most disturbing item of the three are the bones. The coins and watch should be self-explanatory. Years ago, my wrist was shot in the battle of Manassas. It became gangrenous and required the doctor take my hand. The loss was devastating. Now only the bones remain to remind me of the weakness of a human body, the cost of loss, and that time marches on without concern for its victims. It seemed only fitting that I hide this relic in the bowels of Ford's Theater now that my age is calling me to the life hereafter to join my lost love—

Robert

THE BANQUET

Sophie Ravine and two dedicated staff members worked tirelessly to compile a list of the most affluent members of the community. Their ambitious goal was to fill each of the thirty-five tables at the Willard Hotel in Washington, D.C. for an exclusive $500 a plate fundraiser, with the hope of receiving additional contributions during the event. The proceeds would benefit the homeless and provide various non-profit organizations with much needed support. At the end of the evening, she would announce her surprise.

The marble pillars, the bronze chandeliers, the brocade curtains, and the accents of white and gold throughout presented quite a grandiose setting. Perhaps a rustic venue would have better suited her cause, but she hoped the attendees would be a bit more generous with additional donations or with higher bids on the silent auction items if they felt at home in their surroundings.

As she scanned the empty room filled with tables, she thought she saw a musician sitting alone in the corner on the piano bench. She soon realized that couldn't be right. All the musicians were men. This person appeared to be a woman sitting and twiddling her fingers. After moving closer, she discovered it was her teenage niece.

"Hello, Meredith. Where are your parents?" Sophie inquired.

"They're in the lobby with my brother. His babysitter couldn't come. Mom said I have to help you. Honestly, I'd rather be with my friends. They're going to the movies."

"I understand. Except I see your parents' point of view, too. The cause we are supporting tonight is important. I'm sure you can go out with your friends another time." Sophie was firm on this subject and wouldn't allow Meredith's pouty eyes and scrunched lips sway her.

Without further hesitation, Sophie put Meredith to work. "Check the place settings." She gestured across the room with a broad sweep of her hand.

"All the place settings?" Meredith grimaced and paused. "And the chairs?"

Sophie stood with her hands on her hips. "The chairs. Ah, yes, if they aren't centered on the plates, please fix them as well."

"The staff should do this," Meredith complained with an eye roll. "This place is, like, way too flashy. Everyone's going to be decked out in their designer gear. Since I couldn't go out with my friends, I'm here to learn how to be a fundraiser, not a waitress. This is ridiculous."

"Consider this part of your education. Please just make the adjustments wherever they're needed."

Sophie glanced toward the silent auction table, which stretched along the thirty-foot wall of windows. The donated items were impressive. All-inclusive vacations provided by cruises and tour companies, a week at someone's timeshare in Hawaii, wines and whiskeys, handmade professional quilts, a secluded expedition on a sailboat, paintings, sculptures, tickets to major league sports events and theater performances, and jewelry.

Sophie continued explaining. "When you're finished with that, please make sure each auction item has a bidding clipboard and pen in front of the item. My office assistant put them all out, but she had a family issue to deal with and had to rush off. She'll come back with a bundle of press releases by the time dessert is served. Densie, Ali, and Mary will help her distribute them when I'm half way through my speech."

"Yes, I see." Meredith abruptly slid the piano bench back, and stood up.

"I'm not sure you do." Sophie leaned in and kissed her on the cheek and embraced her in a warm hug.

"You're just nervous and giving me extra stuff to do," Meredith said while wrapped in Sophie's arms, and then stepped away.

"Maybe so. Regardless, please try to be more pleasant with everyone. No one else should see this side of you. As a matter of fact, you shouldn't treat me this way either. This event will be a major turning point for many of us."

"Sorry, hormones."

"Yes, well, we all have those to control." Sophie scowled. "I have to go over my introductory speech again. When this evening is over, our lives will go in a different direction."

"What?"

"You'll see," Sophie said. "You can spend the evening at the event or in one of the hotel rooms upstairs until dessert. But I want the entire family here for my speech."

Sophie turned away from her disgruntled niece. Her nephew was so close, she nearly fell over him. The expression on his six-year-old face was pitiful. His elbow appeared to be scraped, and droplets of blood were emerging. A tear ran down his face.

"Meredith, please look after him tonight." Sophie kissed the little boy's head.

"Noooo—Aunt Sophie. May I have some Bactine® and a bandage?" He choked out an unnatural cough and another tear trickled down his cheek. "I hate winter. I want to go back home. It's warmer there."

Sofie consoled him and glanced beyond Meredith at their father. Sophie's brother, Phil. He was standing by the main door. With long strides, he crossed the room.

"You'll be fine, son." Phil took a miniature first-aid kit out of his pocket and doctored the wound. "Pull yourself together. You need to be brave."

"Okay, Daddy." Sniffing, Phil's son dried his tears and puffed out his chest. Together, they walked away. Sophie couldn't help but smile at the two of them. They were so much alike.

Striding up to the front of the room with determination, Sophie reached into a box and brought out a small green tablecloth to add to the already covered table next to the podium. She draped the green one over the larger, crisp white one. With precision, she added an empty plate, glass, and silverware. It looked aesthetically pleasing at first glance. However, unlike the other larger tables in the room, this plate and glass would remain empty as a symbol of food insecurity. This gesture reminded her of a tilted chair in remembrance of lost lives. The chair was for the soldiers she'd known, not for the hungry. That was another lifetime ago. No, she mustn't think about this now. She added a card noting the intention of the table and a stack of fliers listing the non-profit organizations she endorsed.

The two private security guards by the entrance door gave her a glimpse of what life might be like when she proceeded with her grand plans. She pulled the paper out of her pocket and smoothed the creases away. The weight of the words lay heavily on her mind. She read them quietly, expecting no one to eavesdrop. Yet, a member of the waitstaff passing behind her snickered and stepped away. Maybe his behavior was unrelated, but she took it to heart. This was the first time she'd thoroughly reviewed the script, and it came up short. She meant it to be bolder, to leave an indelible mark on the guests. She had thirty minutes remaining to update her speech before everyone entered from the room where the attendees were all enjoying appetizers and drinks at the open bar. Her stomach grumbled from not eating since breakfast, but she refused to surrender to the plates of vegetables, shrimp, and cheeses. The main meal would have to be enough. Even so, she wasn't sure eating would be agreeable.

In a panic, she coaxed long breaths through her parted lips to slow her rapidly increasing heart-rate. This mini-crisis temporarily overwhelmed her—*computer, computer, where is it? Ah, the podium.*

I can fix this with a few word changes and additions. No, I need a second pair of eyes. Wait—I have a solution—where is he?

She grabbed her laptop computer and rushed into the lobby. *Maybe he's here. No—perhaps the room where the appetizers are being served. Hurry, hurry—yes.* "My savior, there you are." Sophie clutched onto his left elbow and whispered in his ear. "Sorry to interrupt your hobnobbing. This speech needs some help."

"Yes, yes. Alright." Her husband, Tom, looked momentarily confused but then complied willingly, even though it had been at least half a dozen years since he'd been involved with speeches. He withdrew from the conversation with the director of the Corcoran with an apology. Sophie guided Tom through a maze of ambling hotel guests in the main lobby while he read the printout. One of the guest services desks was vacant. Tom got busy.

"Thank you, thank you, Tom."

"I can do this, no problem. The meat in the middle is fantastic. The first and last sections need tweaking. They lack punch. I remember you said you only wanted to speak for about three minutes on this one."

"Oh, yes, right."

"I want people to remember you in a positive light."

"Me too." Sophie grimaced and thought of a light bulb to humor herself. "Failing would leave an embarrassing scar."

"You've dealt with worse," Tom said.

"Talking about ways to help the homeless and then making my big announcement might be too much of a surprise for the guests."

"No, no, it's perfect in this context." Tom sighed. "Give me ten minutes alone. I'll fix this."

Sophie took the cue, left the lobby, and went back into the Willard Room. *I need to re-check the tables.* She stopped at each one, moving a fork or plate a fraction of an inch. *Good, good, everything is in place.*

It was time. She breathed a heavy sigh and hoped for a successful event as the attendees strolled in wearing suits, tuxedos, and glitzy gowns, as Meredith had predicted and Sophie had known all along. They carried drinks in one hand and invitations in the other noting, not only the location and admittance into the event, but the specifics of the auction, the time dinner would be served, and the time of Sophie's speech. With a nervous tug, she pulled down the corner of her suit jacket to make certain the stain on the front of her trousers didn't peek out. She'd blotted out the drop of wine that had spilled in their hotel room upstairs, but the area was still damp.

When the security guards opened the doors, the body heat that came with the sizable crowd was palpable. Sophie was relieved she'd taken an allergy pill ahead of time. The smell of cologne and perfume was overwhelming. Some participants made a beeline to their seats, while others lined up along the silent auction tables. Each participant moved back and forth between the items with pens in hand, scribbling down their names and bids. They were like vultures moving in for the kill when someone else added a bid under their names. Each time a bid was adjusted, they would refresh their offer to a higher level. The auction would close just before dessert, and the highest bidder would walk out with their prize at the end of the event after leaving their payment with Sophie's assistant. This was another way to ensure no one would rush off after their main meal.

The people who stayed at the dining tables during the auction seemed more interested in chatting with their neighbors while they waited for the salmon, asparagus, roasted potatoes, and lobster salad. In the meantime, Sophie spotted her dearest friends dispersed by design in various areas of the room. They were also well-known philanthropists who had agreed to help distribute press releases later that evening. There was Ali, whose Mediterranean accent and jovial smile always lit up a room. He wore his customary technicolor patchwork coat, even though Sophie had asked him not to. It was always there except during sweltering D.C. summers. Then there was Mary. She knew how to get anyone interested in anything she had to say because she took a deep interest in what others had to say. And last but not least, cheerful Densie, who always smiled and laughed at everyone's light-hearted stories while sharing meals with them at many events, both private and public.

Sophie milled about the venue, talking to people and encouraging them to place contributions into the decorated cans or hats in the center of each table. This approach wasn't customary for such fundraising events, but it aimed to emulate the items homeless individuals on the streets often used to ask for help. Some had dogs by their sides or played music. The explanation brought nods of understanding. She also encouraged the attendees to stay until the very end of the evening for the surprise announcement during her speech. Only her husband, Tom, and her closest friends knew what she would reveal.

A flock of servers spilled through the doors of the Willard Room and branched out amongst the guests, placing the main course on the tables. The event progressed as planned through the meal and to the end of the auction.

Finally, cake and coffee were placed in front of each guest. The servers exited and closed the main doors behind them. Shortly thereafter, Sophie went up to the podium, placed her speech on the stand, positioned her hands on either side of the paper, then took a deep breath and began—

Good evening, everyone. Thank you for joining me tonight. As I stand before you, I am reminded of a journey—a journey that began with my childhood fears, a journey that led me to become a person filled with hope and compassion. From a tender age, when I walked the bustling city streets with my parents, I was afraid of the homeless. As I matured and saw someone huddled against a building wrapped in a blanket, their haunting murmurs or shouts echoed amongst the cacophony of the city—I couldn't shake the feeling of despair that surrounded them—the psychological torments, the struggles with addiction while knowing they lacked access to proper mental and physical health care.

The institutions of the past were meant to provide care to adrift souls, but instead the places were horrific. While I was relieved, they were closed down in the early 80s, many of the inhabitants were forced to fend for themselves and self-medicate. However, many couldn't manage on their own and didn't have a support system. Apart from these institutions, I learned that becoming homeless or hungry in and of itself can cause mental illness, as was quite evident during the Great Depression. Affluent people, just like us, lost everything and fell into all-encompassing despair.

Recently, I encountered someone who had been caught-up in an abusive family situation. When they sought refuge with friends, they faced a daunting obstacle—their parents, in an attempt to maintain some sense of control, refused to release their birth-certificate which created a labyrinth of complications. Without this fundamental document, it's impossible to get an official ID card or a driver's license or a social security number—a prerequisite to employment. Moreover, it became painfully clear to me that without a formidable set of skills and resources, a person may not be able to get a full-time job that pays a living-wage with adequate health insurance. If all these things work against each other, and if not resolved, this person might be roaming the unforgiving streets in search of sanctuary and a good meal.

This story, sadly, is not unique. Too many people find themselves trapped in cycles of poverty, facing insurmountable bureaucratic barriers to basic necessities. But amidst these challenges, there is hope—hope found in the tireless efforts of modern-day organizations dedicated to assisting the displaced and hungry. These organizations provide vital services—from retrieval of documents, to job training, to mental health support, to housing and sustenance assistance. These organizations are a beacon of hope for individuals and families, offering a lifeline to those in need to help them reclaim their dignity.

The table beside me is empty. But generous organizations fill many tables like this every day. One provides bulk dehydrated food to soup kitchens. Another organization helps with housing so people can rest and shower to prepare for employment interviews. Another organizes job training and placement. The list goes on.

Please consider adding a contribution to the painted cans or hats on your table. Rest assured, every displaced person in America will appreciate the services the money will provide.

Before I conclude, I have an announcement to share—an announcement that underscores my commitment to serve society beyond my years in the military as a JAG lawyer, beyond my years in a private law firm, and beyond my current fundraising endeavors. My announcement tonight is for your ears only until my press conference tomorrow morning at 10 a.m. in this room. You are all welcome to attend. I will be officially launching my campaign for the Presidency of the United States. I believe that together, we can build a future where every American thrives and succeeds.

Once again, thank you all for your support this evening.

An uncomfortable silence hung heavily in the air.

Then…

A roar of clinking glasses followed by applause engulfed the room.

LADY WITH LEGS

A family of four pulled into the damp carpark next to a modest castle with two turrets and shops below. There, the café offered a large English breakfast of eggs, sausage, ham, and toast smothered with kidney beans in tomato sauce.

It was the family's third visit to the small restaurant that week. Before arriving this time, they had gone to the local church to admire the 1810 organ and catch a glimpse of the bells and clock that were installed during Queen Victoria's Jubilee celebration back in 1887. The priest's sermon still lingered in their minds as they stepped out of the car. The air carried a crisp, earthy smell of rain.

"Nice sermon." Stephen broke the silent reflection among them during the drive. He reached his hands to the sky and added an exaggerated yawn.

"Come on, Dad, I'm hungry." Jane pulled on his shirttails.

"The sermon ran a bit long," Midge demurred. "Nothing a coffee and pastry won't fix."

"Maw-m," their youngest—Patty—whined, "What happened to having English breakfast?"

"You all can have mine." Midge moved away from the car. "I'm not in the mood."

They verbally parried back and forth as they walked across the damp carpark. Ducks and doves of all shades freely roamed along the walkways. Their muffled quacks and soft cooing filled the silence. A fair distance in front of them, a woman shuffled toward the café, moving as if the weight of the world rested on her frail shoulders. She didn't bother to pay at the parking machine; her movements were measured but full of quiet determination. Her back was hunched like a vulture, and her eyes seemed to be fixed on something invisible to the observers.

"Should we offer to help?" Jane asked, uncertain.

"Let's wait," Midge replied. "We don't know where she's headed."

"She's scary," Patty mumbled.

The woman's brittle hair hung in limp strands like a dusty old curtain around a face they couldn't quite see. Her legs were bound in thick bandages from the knees down, and her feet were encased in blue and white medical slippers.

"Osteoporosis? Diabetes?" Midge muttered.

"Both, probably," Stephen said quietly.

The skin above the woman's bandaged knees was an alarming shade of cherry-red. She moved with the help of two crane-like canes, which clicked in a consistent tempo against the wet ground. Raindrops formed rings in puddles at her feet and then cleared for her slow but steady march. What took most people two minutes took her a full ten. Someone said good morning to her and held the café door open. The family followed her inside.

When she reached the counter, she set her canes aside and placed her hands on the surface like a tired pianist hitting the keys at the end of a long symphony. With great effort, she straightened her back —though "straighten" might be generous. She gained perhaps a fraction or two of height, an imperceptible victory in her struggle against gravity.

"One coffee, black. 'n' a pastry—whatever's fresh."

The newly hired barista, momentarily caught off guard by the contrast between her frail appearance and firm tone, blinked. "Uh, sure. Do you have a—"

She shook her head. "Nah, no loyalty card today. Just t'coffee 'n' a pastry."

Swiping her card took what felt like an eternity, but no one in line complained. Everyone seemed to understand that time, for her, moved in a different rhythm.

Another worker stepped up. "You all right, Mary? Good homily today?"

"It did go on a bit. The vicar weren't quite 'imself today." She softly cleared her throat. "Still, it's nice t'get out an' about."

After the woman made her purchase, she hobbled to a table with her fists clenched around her two canes. The moment she sat down, her hunched posture dissolved, as though the chair itself had the magical ability to straighten her out. Her face, now visible, was etched with deep wrinkles. Her cheeks were generously rouged, and her lips were painted a bold, defiant red.

"Look at her," Patty whispered. "She looks different now, almost… regal."

Her coffee and pastry vanished swiftly into her cavernous mouth, as if consumed by some unseen force. Not long after, she was back on her wobbly legs, shuffling toward the carpark with several ducks waddling behind her. Their presence added a strange elegance to the woman's movements. The family watched through the café window while they finished their meal. To their surprise, the woman paused beside their SUV and tried the front door, but it was locked. They all rose in unison and then sank slowly back into their seats when the woman moved on. Next, she stopped in front of a small gray car, opened the door and peered inside. She reached into her coat pocket and pulled out a small parcel, wrapped in crinkled brown paper and tied with a wide, faded ribbon. With shaky hands, she carefully placed the gift on the dashboard. For a moment, she stood there, as if lost in thought, before gently closing the door.

"Did she just leave a gift?" Jane whispered, puzzled.

"Looks like it," Midge replied, frowning. "Could be waiting for someone."

The woman shuffled to the next vehicle. This one seems to suit her better. She climbed in and drove away without a second glance.

"Wait—which one of those is really her car?" Jane asked.

"Guess she has options." Stephen laughed.

About ten minutes later, a young man came out of the castle and walked briskly through the rain-soaked carpark. He headed straight for the gray car, hopping in with an ease and energy that sharply contrasted with the woman's earlier struggles. He rubbed his scalp before picking up the package and stroking the faded ribbon with his fingers.

"What do you think it is?" Patty said.

"Who knows," Midge replied, smiling. "A message, perhaps. Or maybe it's a little gift of magic."

The man flipped the gift over in his hands again, placed it back on the dashboard, and drove away.

THE WIGGLYNOSE'S CHRISTMAS IN WALES

Long ago, a family of rabbits named the Wigglynoses inhabited an English churchyard nestled in the countryside. They had made their home in a cozy, warm warren tunneled beneath a weathered statue of the Virgin Mary, which stood silently in the overgrown churchyard of an old abandoned chapel. There were six children: Carly, Bobby, Olly, Penny, Sparky, and Wesley. Almost all the Wigglynose children were well behaved, except for Wesley. He was known for his boundless curiosity and mischievous spirit, and often disobeyed his parents by sneaking into the chapel. The ancient weather-beaten door hung on one hinge and was never fully closed. The gap tempted him. Each time he slipped through the opening, he thought, *Why shouldn't I explore?* His inquisitive nature always won.

Wesley preferred exploring when no one was there. The chapel was a place of contrasts, where the grandeur of the past lingered in the intricate carvings and arches, but neglect had taken its toll. The light filtered through the dust-covered stained-glass windows, casting a kaleidoscope of colors that danced like restless spirits across the dusty floor. Cobwebs draped from the ceiling like tattered curtains, and spiders spun new webs in every corner, their delicate threads shimmering faintly in the dim light. Wesley found the silent vigil of the spiders over the abandoned sanctuary unsettling.

Sometimes, birds fluttered around the altar, their wings beating against the stale air, adding to the eerie atmosphere. These were reminders that this place, once regularly filled with worshipers, now belonged to the creatures of the earth.

But sometimes, people came.

He'd seen them visit the churchyard and occasionally enter the chapel. Their presence was a rare but jarring interruption to his daily routines. Wesley always stayed just out of view while watching them, with a mix of curiosity and fear. Some visitors were scarier than others, especially when they ventured inside. Their voices echoed off the crumbling stone walls like distant thunder to Wesley's ears. He hid in the shadows while watching families with young children, boisterously bouncing off the walls, and older couples, who reverently walked hand-in-hand down the aisle. Wesley imagined himself scurrying beneath the pews, his paws skittering across the cold, worn stones. He knew every crevice and hollow, and when the sun was just right, he could watch the dust float like tiny ghosts in the beams of colored light. The thought of being seen—or worse, caught—sent shivers through him, and he'd shrink deeper into the gloom, waiting for the chapel to be his again.

As frost began to coat the yard each morning, the chapel's air smelled faintly of snow. Wesley's world began to shift. The holiday season was approaching.

When Wesley arrived back at the warren one chilly evening, his family was gathered around the fire, enjoying the warmth.

"Wesley!" his mama scolded. "Where have you been? We were starting to worry."

"Sorry, Mama. I wasn't far. Time ran away with me." At that moment, Wesley decided to temporarily pause his explorations. His family expected him to be present more often at this time of year.

In his deep, gentle voice, Papa said, "Santa Rabbit watches us all the time, but especially this time of year."

"But Papa, does it count if we are good most of the time?" Wesley asked.

"That is not for me to say," Papa replied.

When it was time for Wesley and his siblings to go to see Santa Rabbit, their hearts were racing with anticipation, and they could barely contain their excitement. It would take them a good half hour to hop across the field and through the woods to get to Santa Rabbit within the Bethel Community. No one knew how far away he had to travel from home to visit every child across the rabbit world, or how he managed to speak with each of them.

Waiting in line was almost too much for them. They hopped up and down in place. When their turns finally came, they each told Santa Rabbit what they wanted and if they had been naughty or nice. To everyone's astonishment, when Wesley's turn came, he admitted he'd been naughty and had not behaved in the way his parents wished.

"Try harder," Santa Rabbit said, and pulled a small bell out of his pocket. "Wesley Wigglenose, take this as a reminder. Every time you hear it ring, think of what it means to be kind and careful, even when you are alone."

"Thank you, Santa. I will try." Wesley did as he was told. The bell jiggled softly as he jumped up and down behind his family. The sound echoed in his ears.

As soon as the family hopped back into the churchyard, they found their Christmas tree using their noses. The air was thick with the scent of pine. The tree had grown a few inches over the previous year and now stood two feet tall. Everyone, except Wesley, helped place the trinkets and baubles they had collected over the years onto the delicate branches. When they were done, he jumped up and landed sideways on the tree. Lickety-split, the ornaments popped off. Many of them were broken and beyond repair.

Their father, normally a patient and gentle soul, was furious. "Wesley, you are out of control. Go find pretty things to replace the ones you broke." He pushed Wesley towards the wild woods. "Come back before it's dark."

Reluctantly, with his head held low, Wesley obeyed. He

returned hours later with new decorations for the branches that were not as beautiful as the ones he had destroyed, but adequate enough to restore some of the tree's festive charm. While his brothers and sisters happily arranged the presents they had made for each other around the base of the tree, Wesley, unable to resist, nudged them this way and that, attempting to disrupt their activity. Their parents had reached their limit and sent the children off to bed without singling him out.

Wesley lay awake, his mind racing with thoughts of Christmas and the presents he might receive. Unable to resist, he quietly made his way out of the warren, back to the Christmas tree. There he waited in the cold night for what felt like an eternity for the rabbit in the red jacket and trousers. Santa Rabbit finally appeared with a sack of beautifully wrapped gifts. Each labeled with the name of a Wigglenose rabbit.

Santa uttered his customary jolly laugh that rang through the night. He turned to face Wesley, and his laugh turned into a serious frown. "You have been naughty again." He picked up two presents, showed Wesley the labels, and took them away without another word. Wesley's chest tightened. The weight of his actions began to sink in. Wesley might not be receiving any gifts on Christmas morning. Tears welled up in his eyes. He crawled back into the warren and hoped he was dreaming and hadn't see Santa Rabbit at all.

In the morning, everybody woke up and hopped out to the Christmas tree. The youngest rabbits shouted with delight over the presents they saw. All the boxes had a tag attached with their names and were signed by Santa Rabbit. There were none for Wesley from anyone. Unable to bear the disappointing reality, he bolted out of the churchyard and into the woods, his tiny feet kicking up the old fallen leaves. Mama came up behind him and gently grabbed him by the scruff, pulling him close.

"Son," she said softly, her voice filled with both sadness and understanding. "I'm sorry to say, I don't think you should get any presents because of what you did to the tree. Christmas is a time for extra kindness. If you behave better all next year, I'm sure you'll receive many gifts."

Wesley, his nose scrunched up in frustration, screamed in a shrill rabbit voice, "I can't wait until next year! I must have them now!"

His mama sighed and looked into his eyes. "But Wesley, if you act this way, you'll be unhappy all your life. You must follow the rules. It was wrong of you to break our ornaments. Come on." She coaxed. "Let's go home."

"Yes, Mama." He sniffed. "I shouldn't have knocked the ornaments off on purpose."

When they returned to the churchyard, Mama said, "Now, wash your little furry face and go play nicely with your brothers and sister." He hesitated, and she continued, "Go on, Wesley. You still have time to make things right."

Wesley sniffled again and wiped his tears with the back of his paw. "Oh, all right. I'm sorry." His ears unnaturally drooping down the side of his face in genuine remorse, he hopped slowly back to his siblings with his head hung low. But as he got closer, the familiar sound of them laughing and playing reached his ears, and a small smile tugged at the corners of his mouth. He promised himself he'd try to be a better rabbit, though deep down, he still yearned for thrills and the mischief they would cause. He wiggled his nose, joined the others, while plotting new adventures in his mind, but this time, he would try to be a little less naughty—or so he hoped.

GIRL IN THE CHAIR

The constant reminder of Cassandra's paralyzed legs greeted her each morning. Pulling them out of bed, using the bar that hung across the sheets and over her head, was her only way out. Living alone, she was spared the embarrassment of a close friend witnessing her struggles to get dressed and go out into the world. Even so, she was grateful her brother had retrofitted everything after the accident.

The attention she received during her days in the hospital and subsequent months in the rehabilitation facility were both appreciated and despised. Some days, being human felt burdensome. The years she had spent swimming and running were now confined to the realm of nostalgia, unattainable and surreal, becoming infested within her nightmares. The life from "before" seemed idyllic, and the prospect of returning to it remained an elusive fantasy. The therapist said she could swim again using her arms and a hip floater, but running wouldn't be possible even with the new robotic assistance devices.

Every morning, Cassandra would gaze at her reflection in the mirror. The two-inch streak of silver hair on top of her head shouted at her between the rest of her thick black hair. The contrasting colors felt like a mark of unwarranted shame that reminded her of a skunk that in no way reflected her personality. Instead, it stood as another tangible reminder of the accident that left her skull and soul scarred. Rationally, she knew she should feel grateful for never being in a coma and only suffering from a long gash caused by flying glass, but emotions often overruled logic. On tougher days, the mirror bore the brunt of her inner turmoil. She would fight against the urge to shatter it, wishing to erase the evidence. She resisted, knowing the broken glass would multiply her problems. Instead, on those days, Cassandra would extend her hand across the narrow counter, spray shaving cream onto the glass, watch it foam, and smear it around in a ritualized motion. Over time, this practice had formed a milky film across the mirror's surface. On better days, she would clear a circular space among the dried cream film to apply makeup to enhance her good features and conceal the scars before venturing into public view. With the makeup and her customary black attire, she tried to pretend they were part of a costume of armor to hide her true despair. Still, no matter how hard she tried, maintaining the facade of normalcy was a futile endeavor. She'd thought about moving, but leaving behind the flat where she and Andrew had lived didn't feel like the right answer. The memories would follow her no matter where she was, so she stayed in place.

Simple tasks that had once been taken for granted now demanded an extraordinary amount of effort. Even personal hygiene had become a challenge, despite the modifications made to her flat, including an easy-access shower. The kitchen counters and cabinets had been modified for her disability, so she could cook her own meals, but she couldn't do her own laundry or cleaning. Hiring a person to clean all the surfaces and deal with the washing was a necessity that annoyed her. Leaving her flat had become a self-imposed necessity, even on rainy days.

Riding on the London Tube to work four days a week was part of her routine, with her small backpack always securely positioned by her hip in the wheelchair. The chair she relied upon had become an extension of herself, an intimate connection that no outsider could infringe upon without her consent. She never went anywhere without her backpack containing essential items. A pack of tissues, hand sanitizer, ChapStick™, a wallet, collapsible crutches, and diaper pads for toileting, in case a needed public bathroom didn't have handicap bars. That process was problematic but not as bad as having to use her crutches to maneuver up and down stairs to get to a toilet. Over time, her physical strength had increased from the effort of lifting herself in and out of bed and the wheelchair. The last indispensable item in her bag was a mobile phone, not only for the Toilet Finder app and everyday calls but also for the comfort of knowing it could be a lifeline in an emergency.

Getting through the Tube station had only recently become routine after months of anxiety and uncertainty. The main stations had elevators, others did not. Whenever she had to alter her normal routes, she had to check online to see if handicap resources were available.

She swiped her card over the pedestal, the gates opened, and she rolled through into the cavernous area. The place was so familiar that she could have traveled over to the lift blindfolded. There was no one else nearby, so she moved parallel to the wall and pushed the call button. The doors opened. She rolled over the gap into the compartment and headed down a level to the train platform. The elevator doors opened, and she rolled to the edge of the track. In the back of her mind, she feared falling into the abyss and onto the tracks if her chair didn't stop automatically before it reached the edge. In truth, she always managed to stop it on the correct side of the yellow painted safety line. When she'd started to learn the technique, it was difficult and almost not worth the effort of going into the world. At that point, everything was such a challenge, and life almost seemed not worth living. Since then, living had become a duty, a promise to Andrew and herself. *If one of us should ever die before the other, the one remaining should strive for a full life without regrets.*

Soon, the train streamed into the station with the wind thumping along its sides before coming to a full stop. When the door opened, the train and platform didn't always match up. During those times, a conductor would bring a ramp for her to cross over onto the train.

On this day, she'd rolled right into the handicap area on the train, where there wasn't a passenger seat. She locked her wheels and thought about how this particular day had started. She'd gotten dressed and been eating her breakfast when a random song started playing on the Alexa app. It was an existential moment since she no longer sang or listened to music without tears running down her face. Andrew was dead, and that could not be undone. She had to stop lamenting the loss and strive toward the promise, even though it felt insurmountable. The distracting thoughts didn't help, so she turned on the news on her phone, put in her earbuds, and placed her mobile on the window ledge. Five stops later, she rolled off at a station, leaving her mobile behind.

Bonnie strolled into the Tube station with her four-legged service companion. George stepped over the gap between the platform and the train without concern. She sat in an aisle seat with George snugged up against her leg, just two rows behind an open floor area designated for wheelchairs or bicycles. The train took off, and Bonnie scanned the area for interesting or suspicious characters. Everyone seemed self-absorbed or glassy-eyed. The only exception was the artist, Devon Rodriguez, capturing a man's heavily tattooed face on his drawing paper. The man seemed oblivious to the invasion until the artist spoke to him and presented the rendering. At first, the tattooed man appeared stunned, but then his face lit up with a broad smile and words of gratitude.

Three stations later, Bonnie noticed a woman in her thirties with chalk-white skin maneuvering her wheelchair into position. The chair obeyed hand and voice commands, its black and silver frame mirroring her attire. She was thin, almost anorexic. There was something familiar. The site prompted Bonnie to think about AI robots of the future. They might be a curse or a blessing, depending on the situation. She worried they would be far more intrusive and not as helpful as a wheelchair or automatic lawnmower. Androids like the ones in *Star Trek,* or flying autonomous cars from *The Jetsons* might be fine until one of them went haywire.

Coming back to the current time, Bonnie realized she was hyperfocused on the woman with unblinking eyes. Self-conscious, she looked away, then slipped on her lightly tinted sunglasses, keeping the woman in view while scanning the rest of the train. Not long after, the train screeched to a stop. The passengers parted to allow the woman to roll off the train onto the platform.

Bonnie realized too late that the woman's mobile was still on the ledge. She grabbed the phone and tried to catch her, but the meandering crowds blocked Bonnie's progress. George added to the difficulty of getting through the throngs of people, as they were more inclined to stop and smile at George to admire his sleek coat and excellent manners before allowing them to continue on. Their approval and idle conversation slowed her progress. There could be no denying that a well-groomed and happy Golden Retriever was easier on the eyes than a wheelchair, but Bonnie still needed to move ahead. After a significant number of delays and "please don't touch the dog, he's working" remarks, they escaped the underground tunnels. Outside, Bonnie saw the woman next to a bus working with the driver to get her wheelchair onto the automatic lift. Bus number nine. Bonnie's lucky number. Running to catch it with George by her side, she missed this chance as well. She pulled up short and regained her breath.

Turning the phone in at the station would have been so much easier and efficient. Pushing the thought aside, she hailed a taxi to pursue the bus. As the car passed various streets - Thistle Bridge Drive, Queen Elizabeth Drive - Bonnie kept her eyes peeled, hoping for a glimpse of the woman. Why did she bother to pay attention? Why had this task become so important to her? This was a silly question because Bonnie noticed everything and everyone whenever she stepped out her front door. It had become a habit after she'd been robbed. One could never be too careful about their public surroundings; this she had learned against her will twelve months before.

Bonnie had almost given up when she saw the woman in front of the grocers. She told the cabbie to pull over. By the time she'd paid and exited the vehicle with George, the woman had vanished. After considerable thought, Bonnie breached her rule of never looking at another person's mobile and tapped the screen. It lit right up without a security password. She selected the last number. Three rings later, a man answered.

"Hay, sis, you all right?"

"Um, not her, name's Bonnie. She left her mobile on the tube. I tried to catch up, but she's quick."

"No surprise there. I'm Donnie. Where are you?"

"In front of Sainsbury's Local on Smithfield Road."

"Right, that's on the way to her workplace at Mungos." He provided the address.

"Never heard of it."

"They help the homeless. Guessing you're not." He paused. "Right, love, thanks for the call. If you have time, can you go over? Cassandra would really appreciate a 'good Samaritan' gesture." He proceeded to give her directions to the place, which was only a few blocks away. Donnie worked there too, but on different days.

"No worries. It's my day off. I was going in that general direction to get a ticket for a show."

"I'm trying to go to *The Play That Goes Wrong,* for tonight."

"Yay, I hear it's a hoot." Bonnie took a moment to decide whether or not to say which one she was going for. "I'm picking up my reserved ticket for *Harry Potter* for this weekend."

"Well done. Enjoy your evening. And thanks again for helping out my sister."

Bonnie clicked off the call and keyed in the address on her GPS to Mungos. The automated voice was too loud. A passer-by glared in her direction. She turned the volume down and held the mobile to her ear. As she walked down the sidewalk hugging the wall, she passed interconnected shops on the first floor of multiple buildings. Her thoughts drifted back to a time when she volunteered during an overnight shift at a different homeless shelter with Annabel in the States. That night, there was another volunteer who was very judgmental and criticized several of the homeless guests behind their backs to other volunteers. At the time, it seemed odd that the person signed up for such a task only to follow-up with snide remarks. The particular person of interest to the volunteer was well dressed and smelled like he'd just passed by a men's cologne counter. Anabell explained to Bonnie, who was a little put off by the woman's remarks, that the guest had settled his troubles with the coordinator's help and had just come from his first day of work. It would take a little time for him to earn enough to get a proper house. In the meantime, he'd been assigned highly discounted counsel housing to move into the next day. Anabel knew all this because she was in-the-know with the higher ups. They could trust her to be discreet and respectful. She dressed down the volunteer a bit, saying, "You don't know the circumstances. If you're worried, go talk to management."

The mobile's automated voice interrupted. "Turn right up ahead." Once the turn was taken, it said, "Mungos. Ten paces ahead on your left."

Inside, Bonnie asked the receptionist if she could deliver the mobile to Cassandra but was told to wait in one of the lobby chairs. Well, Bonnie really didn't want to stick around, but she complied, and George did the same. Only she sat in the chair. He settled down next to her.

Within five minutes, Cassandra appeared with a broad smile on face and stopped directly in front of Bonnie. "Thank you. My brother rang my desk and said you'd be here. I must say, you're familiar to me."

"From the train?"

"Yes, there, but no." Cassandra rolled her wheelchair back a foot. "I think I forgot my mobile because I recognized you—from hospital. I was leaving. You were coming in all bloodied."

"Christ! I don't even remember how I got to hospital." George sat up and nudged her hand. "Settle, George, I'm all right."

"Your dog is tuned in. Sorry, maybe I shouldn't have been so blunt."

"No worries. He's trained to sense my moods and alert me to people coming up behind me. I got lucky, and a service dog became available quickly. It usually takes months."

"I've taken up a lot of your time. Maybe I'm overstepping, but do you want to go next door for a coffee?"

"Yay, al'right. It's my day off. Why not?"

Bonnie and George went through the doorway and held it open for Cassandra. At the coffee shop, they went through the same process. Inside, they ordered coffee and went over to a table. Bonnie sat in an existing chair, and Cassandra positioned herself at the end where there wasn't a chair.

"Your name is beautiful."

"Thank you. I was named after Jane Austen's sister. Mum loved the stories at the time." Cassandra's chest rose and fell in an exaggerated fashion. "So, what happened to you?"

Bonnie stroked George's ears before explaining. "I was walking in the park at dusk. Someone grabbed me from behind. The rest is blank until I woke up in the hospital in pain. Turns out I'd been stabbed and robbed. The thief left my wallet behind, so the doctors were able to identify me.

"Blimey. Not a good time for either of us. Your family must have been worried sick."

"My parents are in the States. They didn't find out right away because I didn't have any emergency contacts on me. I called my local friends when I was able, and they came by the hospital. I've never told my parents because they'd likely badger me until I went back to them. Instead, I deferred my Uni exams for a few weeks, found George, and then a job."

"It's good you're all right now. As for me, eighteen months ago, I could walk and I didn't have any grey hair. Got that after it grew back after they shaved it and stitched me up. I had a piece of glass stuck in my head." Cassandra blew on her coffee a few times before taking a sip. "My story didn't involve an attack. Andrew and I were taking a delayed honeymoon. He'd hired a driver to take us to an estate in the countryside with our favorite music playing in the background. Half way into the trip, I remember the driver swerving and a crunching sound. Later, a witness said the car flipped. I ended up like this. The driver tried to save Andrew, but he bled out…"

The shop door opened. "Hello. Sis, great, you two found each other. I presume you're Bonnie?"

"Looks that way. Hello."

"Donnie," Cassandra said. "You checking up on me?"

"Nah. I'm coming with three tickets to *The Play That Goes Wrong*. You two want to go tonight? My treat."

"It should be mine since I've caused all the trouble with my mobile."

BENEATH THE RATTLING ROOF

Our thirty-foot camper loomed in our rearview mirror. It creaked, swayed and groaned in the wind as we headed over the mountains of Utah toward Wyoming on the curving switchback roads. Majestic peaks, dusted with snow, soared in the distance, their silhouettes jagged against a sky that alternated between brooding gray and brilliant blue. On one side of us a twenty-foot drop-off to doom amongst rocks and shrubbery, where sparsely patched wildflowers also clung to life, splashing colors of purple and yellow against the rugged landscape. On the other side, towering, ragged, red- and sand-colored cliffs streaked with veins of ancient minerals hemmed the road.

Slowly, we moved forward. Thankfully, I was not driving. I needed to intermittently keep my eyes squeezed shut. Outside, the wind shrieked like a banshee, tearing through the narrow canyons and whipping up eddies of dust that danced across the road. I took long, deep breaths and attempted to imagine a calmer countenance rather than a panicked one that could send me to the emergency room. There were no medical facilities of any kind in the mountains, few pull-offs and fewer people. I didn't have to concern myself with the altitude. I'd lived up at 7000 feet for several years, and the thinner air no longer affected me.

At the top of a crest, we stopped for a break. The wind was howling at a rate that grabbed the truck door when I opened it a crack, and then closed it with a herculean effort. I tried to steady my panic and go for a second round. I made it out onto the asphalt road and headed towards the camper. When I unlocked the door, the wind grabbed hold and banged it against the side wall. I wondered if it would fly off and take me for a ride like Dorothy's house in *The Wizard of Oz*. The thought was absurd, yet I could almost imagine such an event. Again, all my strength was required to pull the door shut behind me.

The table, once anchored to the floor, had roamed a few feet out of place. The interconnected recliner had slid across the carpet. A better look revealed a three-section unit instead of one. On a calmer day, I decided I'd remove the middle section and change it into a friendlier loveseat to watch television, although the TV set, with its old black-and-white screen, did not work well even on a good day. We decided the amplifier with a DVD slot and the radio were broken. The warranty had run out. Upon reflection, we realized it hadn't worked the day we bought the camper either; DOA. We didn't watch shows too often in our house, even less on the road, except on sweltering evenings when we were exhausted. Outside, the wind continued its relentless assault, rattling the windows as if some restless spirit wanted to come inside.

Looking around more while the wind howled, I saw the baby slide-locks had held most of the cabinet doors closed, except for one. On the floor were bowls, cups, and bananas. I focused on these things rather than the camper's wind induced tremors. The smell of ripe bananas mixed with the faint, lingering scent of the coffee we'd brewed that morning created a strange, comforting aroma that grounded me in the midst of the chaos.

The bathroom was my goal. The struggles I'd encountered to get inside made me believe relieving myself by the side of the road might have been a better choice, except for the terrifying, howling wind. Once I reached my target, I sat and focused on the shower doors. They are convex and initially refused to stay on the manufactured tracks due to a defect in the rollers. Before our trip began, we'd ordered new parts twice. Each time, they were different and dysfunctional. Even during the peaceful drives, the doors fell off.

Adding a bungee cord helped them stay somewhat upright during this climb. When I stood with effort, the wind rattled the camper again. It felt as though the entire structure would, at any moment, become suspended between heaven and earth. I grabbed the sink to steady myself; it worked fine. After the journey to and from the truck, I was eager to get out of the blustering mountain winds to a calmer place.

Miles down the road, the wind velocity diminished, and the camper stopped rattling and shaking. The panic I felt dissipated.

It never ceases to amaze me when I think of the amenities our camper contains. Two propane fireplaces, a full kitchen and bathroom, and a television screen. The only thing missing was a barbecue grill, so we bought one. Upon opening an external compartment and stuffing it in, we soon noticed the floor of the camper was flooding. Initially, a mystery. We pulled the new grill out and discovered it was the culprit. It had turned on a faucet in the closet. The nozzle was side-ways and missed the drain. Hence, the water flowed into the camper and across the floor.

This trip, this first long trip, living on the road for only three weeks, was a novel experience. From the first day to the last, we continually adapted to living in a camper. When we parked for the night at a site and didn't level the floor with jacks, the door wouldn't close with a gentle touch. We had to slam it. The noise seemed to disturb us more than anyone else. Other campers had cats meowing and dogs barking. Still others had barbecues running, which filled the air with either the smell of charcoal or wood smoke mixed with an occasional whiff of grilled meat.

At some camping stops, we could only get 30-amp instead of 50-amp circuits, which affected our water heater and air-conditioning units. We could only run one or the other at a time. Funny, really, since decades ago we were satisfied with tents.

That night, after we made camp, we found a way to have an outdoor fire in an aluminum fire-pit instead of on the ground. The drafts under the flame were so good that there wasn't any smoke swirling around chasing us as we'd encountered in the past.

As the sky darkened, and the first drops of rain spattered against the window, we moved inside.

The camper had all the comforts of home crunched into a box on wheels. No hotels to question their sanitation practices or adjust to a new bed every night. Cooking was easy and healthier than eating out every day. The COVID pandemic was beginning to recede. Our vaccinations were completed before our travels, although our worries remained. As we sat in the camper that night, listening to the rain drum steadily on the roof, it felt like a small haven against the uncertainty that had gripped the world for the past year.

We had hauled the camper across the country to move to Wyoming a year before the world locked-down by degrees. Our adult children left countries abroad to return and hunker down with us in Wyoming. Each one came at different times, and they each quarantined in the camper for two weeks before getting COVID tests to clear them to join us in our house. So, I am thankful for our home on wheels. And now, as the future unfolds, we can travel with caution and see our country in the way we had intended for some of our adventures.

JANE AUSTEN AND THE TRAVELING LAPTOP

Kat stepped off the platform onto the first train she found leading toward her destination—The Jane Austen Festival in Bath, England. She'd traveled over three thousand miles in the last few days. The trip began with a black roller suitcase she'd had to replace because the wheels broke soon after she arrived at her first stop. It was too heavy to carry with her crippled shoulder, and the only available alternative was a conspicuous neon pink one. Normally, she preferred to keep a low profile, but protecting her shoulder took priority.

After repacking everything, she discovered that her custom-made Regency-period hat wouldn't fit in the suitcase, and proved too ridiculous to wear on her head in modern times, so she wound the ribbon around her wrist and took the chance of being questioned about its purpose. Worrying about the pink suitcase seemed superfluous, since the hat with its flowers, feathers, and half-brim stood out on its own. Between the suitcase, the hat, and her laptop satchel, Kat had quite enough to deal with. Staying focused and alert was difficult. Rubbing her eyes every time her eyes tried to close or glaze over didn't help her recover from her exhaustion. She'd only slept a few hours during the past three days.

All she wanted to do was sit down and rest on the train, but she didn't want to settle herself by the first person she came across near the aisle. The last time she'd done so, the business executive turned out to be an evangelist who wanted to heal her by putting his hand on her injured limb. The gesture seemed presumptuous, and she didn't appreciate him intruding on her personal space. Until then, she'd valued their conversation about the positive and negative aspects of spiritual connections to the Great Beyond.

On this train, Kat picked out a woman with short, wispy, gray hair and silver-rimmed glasses. Just for fun, she named her Mildred without asking her real name. Kat lifted her garish pink suitcase onto the luggage rack across the aisle while fumbling to keep her crossover purse in place. With an iron grip on her laptop satchel and a gentler one on the Jane Austen hat, she sat down next to Mildred. The woman smiled and greeted her. Kat couldn't help responding. Her American accent sounded strident and grating in contrast to Mildred's refined, melodic English voice.

Initially, Kat was more interested in watching her suitcase to make sure no one walked off with it. The contents included handcrafted Jane Austen costumes that Kat couldn't replace within the required timeframe. She had spent more than sixty-hours designing and constructing the authentic garments for the upcoming event. Despite efforts to stay alert, it became nearly impossible to keep her eyes open, but falling asleep wasn't an option. No one would wake her at the transfer station. In desperation, she asked Mildred about the crossword puzzle lying in her lap.

"A crossword puzzle from The London Times," Kat stated. "Is it difficult?"

"Oh, yes, dear. Have a look. Pitch in if you like."

About twenty minutes later, a train whizzed by on a parallel track. Kat realized she'd hopped on the slow train when she'd paid for a ticket on the faster train. She brought up this point with Mildred, who had a prompt reply. She explained that the higher priced tickets had not been available the day before because the train was out of service. Because of the circumstances, this was surely a better choice, even though there were more stops and took a little longer. Instead of resuming the crossword, Mildred inquired about Kat's journey. This wasn't the first time someone had asked.

Here we go, Kat thought. *It's time to recite my monologue. I'm in a nasty mood. So tired.* She began. "I came from the States a couple of days ago to see our daughter on the way to the Jane Austen Festival in Bath. The plane flight ended up being an easy hop from Baltimore to Iceland and then to London."

"Aw, London," Mildred interrupted. "I used to live there seven years ago before I moved out of the city to a seaside retirement community." Mildred covered her mouth with her hand for a second. "Sorry, dear, I didn't mean to switch the subject."

"It's all right."

"Go on then."

"After two trains, I arrived at our daughter's home in time for dinner. That night, I received an email with a sales contract to review for our house back in the States. My husband told me to get some sleep, but I was too excited. We'd been waiting a long time for someone to put an offer on the house."

"Congratulations."

"Thank you." Kat smiled and kept talking. Sometimes she didn't know when to stop. "Eventually, I settled down in bed but only slept for two hours. In the morning, I had six coffees and a full English breakfast. I love beans and toast. Not long after, my husband sent me another email saying I should go to the festival. I'd need to cut my other plans short and go home instead of going to Harrogate with friends."

"Oh dear, won't that cost a lot to leave early?" Mildred smiled, and a silver tooth caught Kat's eye.

"No, I bought a one-way ticket to England from the start. Surprisingly, the airline rates matched a round-trip ticket."

"That was lucky." Mildred chimed in with a tone of encouragement.

"Thanks for helping me stay awake. I feel bone-tired from lack of sleep, and I need to transfer over to other train lines that will take me to the Bath Spa station."

"The spa experience is quite relaxing. If you have time, take a soak."

"That's a good idea, but I think I might have too many things scheduled." Kat rubbed her hands together to warm them. "Sorry, I think I'm talking too much."

"It's all right. Let's work on the crossword puzzle some more." Mildred's eyes clenched together, then flicked open. "We have a layover at the same station up ahead. Would you like to share a cuppa?"

Kat paused for a moment, trying to remember what a cuppa meant. A tea and some type of cake. "Oh yes, that would be nice."

Mildred began reading out the crossword clues. "A heavy, horned animal?"

"How many letters?"

She counted with the tip of her pencil. "Ten."

Kat blurted out, "Rhinoceros."

Back and forth, they bantered about the answers. Kat loved the diversion. As the train pulled into the station, Mildred abruptly stopped scribbling answers, folded up the paper, and slid it into her oversized brocade handbag.

Kat collected her cumbersome pink suitcase from the rack across the aisle and rearranged her purse, hat, and laptop satchel on her good arm. They shuffled towards the exit, stepped off the train onto the platform, and hurried into a Gothic-style waiting room. The tea in the shop wasn't strong enough for Kat, but it helped wake her up a bit while they sat on café chairs around a small, circular table. They would go on different trains when the time came to leave. Mildred commented on the towering modern buildings under construction outside the waiting-room window. They both agreed that the older stone buildings with multiple tall and narrow chimneys held much more interest than the glass and steel structures being constructed.

One cup of tea later, Kat switched to coffee. Mildred talked about barges and the adventures she'd had while traveling down the

English canals in years gone by. Kat wondered why Mildred shifted the conversation to canals when there were none in sight, but any subject would do to prevent her from dozing off. About five minutes before the trains arrived, they exchanged contact information and said goodbye. Whether they saw each other again was inconsequential, but she would always remember Mildred's kindness.

The next train was so crowded that Kat almost didn't get a seat on the coach. Thankfully, she didn't have to stand, like many others did. They crammed into the aisle within inches of her crippled shoulder. The pink suitcase had to go between her legs. She wedged the laptop satchel between her chest and the seatback of the person in front of her. In order to prevent the hat from being pancaked, she shoved it on and tied it snugly under her chin, no longer concerned about others' opinions of the ribbons and feathers. The compartment was stuffy, and her head fogged with the lack of air. Smells of sweat and something like an old kitchen sponge gone sour filled her nostrils.

After a time, the crowd thinned out, and the person who had been sitting next to Kat was gone. Her seatmate had struggled to climb over her, but in a comic acrobatic maneuver. She moved the laptop satchel to the newly vacated seat next to the window, pulled a water bottle out of her purse, and drank half of the contents. The fog in her head began to clear, but not enough—not enough. Four stations later, the announcement came; it was time to depart. The train was emptying fast. If she didn't hurry, the door would close, and then she'd have to go ahead to another stop before returning on an inbound train to this station. Meeting her friend Lyn at a specific time was non-negotiable, so she had to get off. With her suitcase in hand, Kat escaped through the door as the chimes warned of the train's imminent departure.

Around a corner, she hustled down the stairs, then up another stairway, to another platform and train. She barely made it through the chiming doors and stood near them rather than going further into the compartment. The train moved ahead a few more stops before she had to exit again.

Outside the train station, she found Lyn and breathed a sigh of relief. She'd hardly said hello when the realization hit her. The panic choked her throat. The laptop satchel was gone. She'd forgotten it in the confusion of the crowded train. How would she find it? She didn't know. In a brief span of time, through two different train companies, she'd bollixed everything up. Venturing alone carried risks, especially when factoring in fatigue. Unaware, she'd left the satchel on the seat. With Lyn's calming influence, they formed a plan.

They made their way over to the 'lost and found' desk at the Great Western Rail. After explaining the situation, the man scribbled something on a piece of paper and handed it over. It explained how to contact the other related train lines. He said that at the end of each run, the conductors walk through the compartments. They clean up debris and lost items, hoping to return the items to their owners. This prospect didn't give Kat much hope. She couldn't imagine that there could be honest passengers who would leave her laptop satchel alone rather than taking it for themselves. She hoped and prayed she was wrong since her tickets for the Jane Austen Festival were in the bag, along with several passwords for various online accounts. The lost passwords concerned her the most. She wouldn't have to worry about losing any money because she could access her reservations for the events at the registration desk in town. When they got to the bed-and-breakfast, she borrowed Lyn's Tablet™ and quickly got online. She was still in such a panic that she couldn't recall anything. A couple of slugs of red wine, along with breathing exercises, soon did the trick. When her nerves were frazzled, she was never good at thinking things through. After contacting her husband to help her use her home computer to access Gmail, she generated a new set of passwords.

Without a doubt, this marked the beginning of a lengthy journey for her unfortunate laptop. Lyn mused that it would likely appear in a few weeks or not at all. Kat felt devastated at the thought of losing such an expensive piece of equipment but also about losing the latest 2000 words of her novel. She backed up her writing frequently, but hadn't done so since her last session. The festival might distract her, but not enough to stop her from worrying about the lost words.

Kat was a neophyte when it came to anything associated with Jane Austen. But she loved costumes and traveling. So, when Lyn invited her to the festival, she had to say yes. Over the years, she'd seen movies inspired by Miss Austen's novels. Yet Kat hadn't read any of the books until months before the festival. She had picked up a copy of the annotated edition of *Emma*, which totaled almost a thousand pages with the notations. After considerable frustration, she watched the film version of *Emma* and listened to the audiobook instead. Both were more enjoyable than slogging through the book she'd purchased.

Wearing period costumes during the event would place her in the proper state-of-mind to fully participate. This was especially true at the dances, which brought to mind contemporary square dancing devoid of the stereotypical American Western attire. The elegance of the women during the event, with their empire waist gowns fitting snugly under the bust line and dropping unimpeded to the floor, would create a floral arrangement of color. Kat was sentimental about the Regency gowns because they reminded her of her aunt, who often wore similar dresses with a single red flower in her onyx upswept hair.

The participants' ages spanned from thirty to seventy, but were primarily women. The few men in attendance wore tight breeches with tailcoat jackets, which added to the fascination of the Regency event. While it was unfortunate that the festival attracted so few single men, neither Kat nor Lynn cared because they had loving husbands at home.

The daily and evening finery, adorned with accessories of hats, gloves, and scarves, created a dandy affair. Some costumes were made by skilled seamstresses, either by participants or artisans. Other garments could have been rented at costume shops, refashioned from second-hand stores, or bought online. Many did not want to reveal their secret stash, but one mentioned she'd made her dress from a shower curtain. The story of *Gone with the Wind* by Margaret Mitchell came to mind. The main character, Scarlet O'Hara, tore down a curtain in her ravaged home after the Civil War and fashioned a green velvet dress out of it. Decades later, one of Carol Burnett's unforgettable comedic scenes of the green curtain dress called "Went with the Wind," complete with curtain rods still attached, brought laughter to Kat's tired body. These women exhibited resourcefulness and determination. Kat hoped to gain some of both.

On the opening days of the festival, all the costumed participants lined up at the Royal Crescent, which was built in the latter half of the 1700s. The thirty townhouses, museum, and hotel are collectively five-hundred-feet long and arc around a green space. The space has two sections divided by a step-down wall that is known as The Ha-Ha. It was designed to keep the livestock away from people enjoying the green space near the buildings. Kat and Lyn gathered with several hundred people preparing to parade, or promenade, through the streets of Bath. Re-enactors of the soldiers of the 33rd Regiment led the group through the streets. On both sides of the road, tourists and locals took photographs of everyone in their Regency finery until the assembly reached the Parade Gardens alongside the Avon River. There was also an opportunity to stop at the Holburne Museum to visit the regiment's encampment along the side of the building.

Each year's festival photographs would appear in the organization's newsletter and in the following year's program announcements. Kat and Lyn hoped their photos would appear. However, they were equally thrilled when a stranger approached them in the Waterstones bookshop and asked if he could take a photo of them while they stood in front of a shelf containing multiple copies of Jane Austen's novels. The women felt like movie stars.

In addition to the dances, many activities related to Jane Austen took place, such as teas, short theatrical performances, and guided walking tours. The program was extensive, but Kat and Lyn weren't going to attend them all during the ten-day period. They planned to take breaks from the events to watch a *Downton Abbey* film, go to a local spa, meander through the Fashion Museum and stroll along the Kennet Canal to see the houseboats, or embarked on a quest to find the best toffee sticky pudding in town.

Despite all the distractions, the lost laptop continued to occupy Kat's thoughts. Lyn suggested a visit to the spas to help her refocus. Kat knew she needed to focus on the local experiences, but couldn't stop herself from brooding about the loss and her foolishness. Still, she grabbed a bathing suit, leaving Lyn behind for a nap, and walked through the town's historic streets to the Thermae Bath Spa. There was a line with an hour's wait. Once she reached the entrance, Kat paid thirty-six British pounds, which gave her two hours of spa time. The staff provided a towel, robe, and flip-flops along with a blue, coded plastic wristband. She walked through a turnstile into a maze of blue barriers to circumnavigate.

Both men and women occupied the same area, with private cubical changing rooms lined up on either side of an aisleway. Kat stepped inside one and closed the front and back doors without understanding how to open them again. Not worrying too much, she changed into her bathing suit in the cramped quarters while wondering how anyone with a large girth could manage. Her troubles compounded when a back spasm came on. Fortunately, it dissipated after stretching in various directions. After balling up her casual clothes and getting ready to leave, she discovered that neither door would open. Claustrophobia seeped into her chest. A few deep breaths later, she composed herself and found the correct handle to escape the cramped quarters.

The next challenge was the lockers. After some effort, she realized there was a scanner to wave her wristband across. Magically, the vacant locker opened and swallowed up her street clothes. The next battle required following the signs up, down, and around to get to an indoor mineral pool for a half hour of floating among artificially created currents. The ebb and flow of the waters further calmed her sore back and drained spirit. After emerging from the water, she proceeded to another level and discovered a wet and dry sauna, along with an ice room. Of course, she had to try them all. In both saunas, sweat dripped down her temples while more erupted across her body. The scent of eucalyptus was infused in both rooms and helped clear her sinuses. Fog poured out of the door of the ice chamber. The room greeted her with a pleasant, cool atmosphere instead of a frigid one. An attendant appeared and explained that rubbing a handful of ice chips on her skin from the trough would produce the desired chill. An ice hotel came to mind, but there were no furs to wrap herself within these chambers.

Kat slept soundly for two hours in the afternoon until the soothing sounds of Beethoven's Sonata No. 27 in E-minor flowed from her mobile phone. When the music began, her dream changed from running to strolling down a road in jeans and a T-shirt. A cord on a brown paper bag pinched her hand and dangled down by her knees. She arrived at a house and went inside without recognizing whose place it was. Everyone else was wearing Jane Austen Regency costumes. She hid in a corner behind a clump of artificial bamboo plants and peered into the bag. To her surprise, there was a costume inside. She put the dress over her t-shirt and jeans, but forgot to take off her hiking boots.

∽

The phone's sonata rose to a crescendo. Responding to the loud sound, she sat up straight and wide-eyed, recalling the dream, and snickered. She mused; *I must have looked like a hillbilly character with those clunky boots. What was the TV show called? Beverly Hillbillies. A country woman failing to fit into high society.* The consequences of leaving the laptop on the train had melded into her mind and subconsciously transformed the anxiety into clothing. When comparing the complexities of extensive outlining and the imaginative process required for writing, the sewing task seemed much simpler. Although her lost writing would go unnoticed during the festival, the absence of appropriate clothing would be quite apparent. The shame of being dressed incorrectly, of being stared at for being different, weighed on her mind. An unusual concern considering she enjoyed being noticed, but only if she dressed and acted correctly in a situation. While she was awake, her costumes were hanging in the wardrobe, and her laptop was missing. The tension she'd experienced when she'd left it behind had subsided out of necessity, but it had resurfaced when she pulled the covers up and closed her eyes.

During the remaining days of the festival, no one reached out with any news about her laptop. With grave disappointment, Kat returned to America.

Three weeks later, Kat heard from the train line. Someone had turned in her satchel and laptop, but there was a hitch. She would either have to pick it up herself, send a messenger, or have it mailed for a hefty fee. The satchel and its contents had made the rounds from Bath in the south of England all the way over to London. She ran her hands through her hair while trying to focus on a solution. After talking to Lyn about the problem, luck would have it that her friend would be traveling to London in the coming weeks. She offered to pick up the satchel and bring it back with her to America. By the end of the month, Kat would have her laptop with her lost words back in her possession. The outcome of her absent-mindedness on the train turned out better than she'd ever hoped. Lyn and the person who turned in her satchel were her heroes.

The day arrived, and the bag returned intact with an extra envelope enclosed. With a sigh of relief, she wondered what kind of adventure the laptop had while she was going on with her life. On the piece of paper inside, she read about the journey of the traveling laptop. It went like this—

Dear Freund,

Mein namen es Jurgen. I am from Munich, and German is my native language. I will write in English. When I found your bag on the train late at night, I was unsure of what to do. Unfortunately, the department for lost articles was closed, so leaving it by the door would have been a mistake, so I took it to my hotel. When I opened the computer, the password protection did not surprise me, but I wished it was not there. The enclosed password notebook didn't help me. It seemed to be in code. I wanted to know what the machine contained. Simply out of curiosity, not to steal or reformat the drive. Inside the satchel, I found tickets for a Jane Austen event and some pages of a short story.

I have visited many places in the world where Ernest Hemingway had gone and learned about the story of his lost manuscript. I don't know if you have heard about this. He had gone traveling and left his most current work at home. His wife found the story on his desk. She put the pages and carbon copies into a satchel to take to him, but in a rush, she left the train without the stories. Maybe this is your situation, too.

I wonder who you are, but I think I will never know. I traveled around the city carrying your satchel. I do not know why I did such a thing. I am not this type of person. The Jane Austen tickets made me think you might be a woman. I found your business card, and your name appears to be German. I planned to bring the bag to the main London station and drop it off so they could get in contact with you. I am sure that is better than doing it myself. I am sorry if I have caused you any trouble. Your satchel has gone to the Portobello Hotel in London, with its beautiful antiques. There we (your laptop and I) met my friends for a business meeting. We also stopped at the Hemingway Bar on Victoria Park Road. Since you are a writer, I guessed you might appreciate knowing these things. I write suspense books. You write literature. It is amazing two writers found each other in this way.

Hopefully, it has not taken too long to be reunited with your laptop. And one day, perhaps, we will meet each other. See the enclosed photograph along with one of my books.

Yours,

Jurgen

Jurgen
Jgen@freenet.com

COFFEE, SMOKE, AND SURPRISES

Maggie hunted for the ringing phone. It was buried under a Smithsonian magazine that she hadn't gotten around to reading. She grabbed the phone and looked at the caller ID. It was her son. The reception wasn't ideal, and his voice sounded like he was talking into a tin can. To keep her other hand busy, she picked up a sponge and wiped down the kitchen counters.

"Let's have breakfast together tomorrow," Joey said.

"Yes, I'd love to," Maggie replied.

"We need to meet at 8 a.m. at the bus stop. My class schedule is packed."

"Which bus stop?" Maggie asked.

She continued wiping down the kitchen counters. Standing still while waiting for anything wasn't one of her strong points.

"Mom, at the usual one." A sound rustled through the phone. "Like I said, my schedule is crazy. We have to meet then."

She couldn't figure out why he sounded so insistent. It wasn't like him, and it was too damn early, but curiosity won out. At the appointed time, they rendezvoused at the bus stop on Connecticut Avenue by the National Zoo. He didn't say much other than greet her with a smile until they reached the university campus. She thought of four years before when he had first chosen her alma mater, and the pride welled up again.

At the corner of H and 21st Street, the bus pulled up in front of an empty lot where a building had stood during her years at George Washington University. A sign announced the future home of a "Modern Luxury Dormitory" built by a construction company she'd never heard of. There was still another building behind the lot, with windows and a back door facing into an area connected to an alleyway. On the other side of the road, the Lisner Auditorium had a renovated courtyard to its right with vibrant flower beds flanking a polished pathway leading up to the shiny obelisk. Back in her day, she'd interviewed people for her psychology class in the same space, but there hadn't been any flower beds there at the time.

Joey's phone chimed. Looking at the screen, his face scrunched up. "Sorry, Mom, I need to step away for a short meeting."

The phone chimed again. Maggie felt rather annoyed by the constant interruptions of text messages; this was *their* time. She didn't want to wait, but also didn't want to go home.

"I'm sorry. I won't be gone long. Let's meet back here at the obelisk in forty-five minutes."

"I'll be waiting. Please don't take any longer."

Joey jogged off with his backpack flopping left and right across his shoulders. He, like most runners, was fit and lean. Maggie longed for the days when she had been in similarly good shape. The years hadn't been kind. Her midsection had lost its definition. She snickered at herself for referring to her own body as *it*.

By the curb sat a vendor's cart with a whistling man helping clients. Steam drifted out of a pot of boiling water. The scent of dark roast coffee mixed with milk captivated Maggie. A black coffee—hold the cream and sugar—would perk her up. The man poured the brew into a to-go cup, and she paid cash while thinking cash might disappear in the future. These days, more often than not, people use a debit or credit card. For small amounts, it hardly seemed worth the effort to pull out her card. She thought back to the times when vendors didn't want cards used for anything less than five dollars because they'd be charged a fee.

Maggie meandered back to the courtyard and sat down on the bench to wait. Looking at the coffee, she smiled and recalled never being willing to buy anything from street vendors or food trucks for fear of getting ill. Now, these fears seemed irrelevant, swept away by changing times. Everyone purchased food without any problems due to inspections and licensing laws. Lifting her toes to the sky, she did a few rounds of leg lifts and breathed in the moist air.

Two other people appeared and sat on the bench on the other side of the narrow courtyard. Both appeared rather placid right up until they began a heated debate on international affairs, which she did everything in her power to avoid listening to. Not only was it rude to eavesdrop, but she'd had her fill of such things on the news the previous night. Among other things, the world was off balance; people were having trouble finding jobs with proper pay and health insurance. Maggie figured technology had become a good and bad thing.

Fifteen minutes later, a commotion began on the opposite side of the street beyond the vacant lot. From the back of the building, smoke billowed out of the upper windows. People were shouting as they ran out the door on the street level. Almost everyone was dressed in robes or pajamas. Maggie wasn't sure whether or not to call the emergency crews. Her fingers hovered indecisively over her phone. The fire alarm was blaring so loudly, she put the coffee cup down on the bench and covered her ears. In those moments of indecision, lights from the sides of the empty lot popped on and began to flood the area with multi-colored beams. People from the nearby apartment buildings rushed down to the sidewalks with chairs and sat down to watch. Others stood. This was the craziest thing she'd ever witnessed. Why were they sitting there gawking and not helping? An ancient fire truck pulled up with two men seated in the front, but they didn't get out or do anything to help. Multi-colored balloons floated out the lower windows of the building. The 'audience' began shouting. Just about the time Maggie thought she'd go mad with anxiety, Joey showed up with Sandy.

"What *is* going on?" Maggie asked, her shoulders stiffening.

"Mom, it's okay," Joey replied. "This isn't real. It's a stage production they brought outside to create something authentic in the actors' minds. Think of it as a flash-mob."

"Well, it worked. I was terrified for the victims. It was shocking. Imagine those people sitting around not doing anything if it were real. I would have preferred watching singing or dancing; thank you very much." Maggie's sarcastic thank you was a British thing she'd picked up after many visits to the UK.

"Never mind them." He put his arm around his girlfriend. "Mom, I had to go get Sandy. I wanted her to have breakfast with us, but she wasn't picking up her phone. The earlier pings on my phone before I left you weren't her—they were reminders. Anyway—we have a surprise for you."

"Really, Joey, I can't take any more excitement today after that fictional fire across the street."

"Mom, you'll be all right."

"Nice to see you again, Mrs. Tilley," Sandy said.

"You too, dear." Turning to her son, she said, "Can we go to breakfast? I'm hungry. Aren't you two?"

"Yes, yes. Mom. But first, we have something big to tell you." Joey clasped and unclasped Sandy's hand in an exaggerated gesture. "We're engaged."

"Engaged for another show?" Maggie teased.

"Mom, really? No, we're engaged." With his free hand, Joey pointed back and forth between Sandy and himself. "Marriage. I asked Sandy to marry me."

"Right on the steps of the Lincoln Memorial. On one knee."

Sandy pulled out her hand, that had been hiding in her jacket, to show off the ring.

"Aw…" She contained her delight and took Sandy's hand. "Congratulations. That's lovely. Mm, looks familiar."

"Mom, you're too funny."

"Who, me?" Maggie hugged them both in a group hug. Stepping back, she said, "So, that's why your dad was asking me where I'd hidden his mother's ring."

SHADOWS ON BRYCE STREET

Elaine drove down a residential road lined with aspen trees. Their leaves fluttered in the fall breeze, glowing with the burnt oranges and yellows of autumn. As a child, she had not known the road's name, but now, after some research, she knew it to be called Bryce Street. As she drove closer and closer, memories washed over her, flooding into the forefront of her consciousness. Elaine couldn't forget how she'd come to live at the Burdock Institute, but the lingering questions—the voids—had shaped her personality and every moment going forward. For years, she had avoided returning in an effort to escape her past, but this year, after dreaming of her childhood, she relented.

Between two houses along the road stood an iron gate with a long driveway leading up to a rough-cut, large stone limestone building, with a small cottage off to the side. A playground with a rusty swing set stood erect in a corner; the swing twitched with the breeze. She pulled into the driveway, stopped in front of the gate and closed her eyes, forcing herself back in time.

A very tall woman by Elaine's standards stood above her four-year-old self. The place looked scary. Her mother, Dee, told her to go play and meet some other children. Mommy Dee said she would be back in three hours. Elaine didn't have a clear concept of time. The other kids were complete strangers. She felt abandoned when Mommy Dee left her at the school. All Elaine could do was hope that she had been left in a safe, trustworthy place. She played with the plastic bucket and shovel in the sandbox and swung on the swing.

Sharing things was difficult since she didn't have any brothers or sisters. Everyone else seemed to know how to handle themselves in a group setting. A little girl with two long, black braids invited Elaine to help build a sandcastle and led her back to the box. They built a two-story castle.

From then on, Elaine was dropped off every morning. Her least favorite thing to do was lay down at naptime with a blanket and pillow. She really hated quiet time; the teacher read them stories from *The Brothers Grimm*. She realized the teacher had altered the stories while reading them slowly, with her voice modulating up and down. The other kids would fall asleep to the teacher's melodic voice. Elaine could not sleep because she had a vivid imagination, and many of the stories scared her. Elaine went on to read them as an adult, all two-hundred, with the convoluted grammatical constructions she found difficult to comprehend.

When Mommy Dee returned at the end of each day, Elaine would run to her and engulf her mother with hugs. She never cried in front of the teacher, but some of the younger kids did from time to time when they were tired or frustrated. If Elaine wanted to cry, she saved her tears for her pillow when she went to her room at night.

As Elaine sat in her car with her memories, she felt a bit hollow inside. The teacher, Miss Jones, was so kind. They'd been together for only half a year when another woman came in as a substitute. When Miss Jones finally returned, she had a metal brace on her leg.

Elaine asked Mommy Dee, "What is it, Mommy?"

Mommy Dee bent down and whispered, "She had polio. I'll explain later." But Mommy Dee never did.

Miss Jones was Elaine's teacher for years in the small school. Eventually, Elaine got two leading roles in the school plays. The first was *Hansel and Gretel;* she was Gretel. The second was a play about Jesus, and she was Mother Mary. Mommy Dee was very proud. Elaine's newfound popularity spurred her on to chase the boys around the playground when she was only eight. She invited her neighbor Enzo to her school's carnival, hoping that he would make her friends and the schoolboys jealous, but it didn't work.

Enzo lived next door. They spent a lot of time together outside because there weren't any other little girls in the neighborhood. Sometimes they'd go into each other's houses, but only when Mommy Dee could divert herself from household chores to supervise. Most of the time young visitors weren't allowed in the house.

On one occasion, they'd gotten into trouble at home. Elaine had made a mud bath in the backyard. She invited Enzo over, and they sat in the mud in their underwear, rubbing the sludge all over their arms and legs. Mommy Dee thought it was cute at first, but she became angry. She wanted to know why they were practically naked. It seemed obvious to them. Elaine had replied politely that she didn't want their clothes to get dirty.

That was the last thing Elaine could remember about her mother. The very next day, she took Elaine to school and never returned. Miss Jones told her that her mother had died in a car accident. They had gone to the funeral together. Everyone wore black clothing and the fragrance of the daylilies stuck in her nose. As an adult, whenever she was around such flowers, she felt nauseous. After the funeral, no one could be found to take care of Elaine. Even so, funds were transferred into a trust to provide for her, with Miss Jones as her guardian. Elaine eventually called her Mommy Claire. They lived together in a cottage on the school grounds until Elaine went off to college and Claire moved to New York City. They wrote or talked on the phone after they parted, but never managed to meet in person again. She thought it was one of those situations where you meet and remember someone forever due to the circumstances without staying involved in each other's lives.

From the driveway, the house looked empty and overgrown, but there was a light on in the attic window and another by the front porch. She thought it looked haunted, filled with memories of the children who had gone off into the world, leaving the house behind. She had taken the memories with her and carried them into her future. With that thought, Elaine put the car in gear. The engine hummed like a comforting lullaby. As she drove away, she vowed never to return. She felt a mix of emotions—relief, sorrow, and a strange sense of closure. The memories of the Burdock Institute, of Mommy Dee and Claire would always be with her, but they no longer held her captive. She was free to create new memories. Unburdened of her past, she embraced the future as if stepping into the light after years in the shadows. The road ahead was uncertain, but for the first time in years, Elaine felt ready to face whatever lay ahead.

WHEN THE SILENCE BROKE

Forty years had passed since they'd split under unusual circumstances. The phone call Catlyn had received just yesterday felt ghostly. The voice on the other end of the line was his—except that didn't make sense. Jody was dead. Or so she thought.

After the call, Catlyn rifled through a box of mementos and found his death notice. It clearly stated the service location and the burial ground. She hadn't gone to either. By then, she'd lived too far away to get there in time. And truth be told, she hadn't believed her presence would help anyone. All she'd done was write a conciliatory letter to his father, noting that Jody's military service and the surrounding events had been the cause. She felt it necessary to say so, since the letter Jody had left behind implied his father's failures—and a breakup with another girl—were the main reasons. She knew otherwise.

But knowing didn't grant her peace. There were events that had occurred during that time that she still couldn't look at directly—stray memories she'd trained herself to ignore. The way Jody had gone quiet in crowds. His sudden disappearances for days at a time. The night he'd cried on her shoulder without saying a word, then kissed her like she was the only anchor he had left.

A response from his father never came. At the time, that silence only added to Catlyn's distress. They had split nearly three years before. The only reason she even knew about his death by suicide was because of a voice message left on her answering machine from Margot.

Catlyn had built a new life since then—a husband, children, and a comfortable home in the suburbs. That chapter had closed, too. She'd lost John suddenly in a road accident five years before. No long goodbyes, no time to prepare. The grief felt easier to explain, but no easier to carry. She'd mourned him with casseroles, sympathy cards, and lonely nights. Jody, she'd mourned in secret.

The reason for their failed relationship had never been fully explained. The end came after a series of events that felt senseless even at the time. Those forty years hovered in her mind and spun out of control. She had boxed up the memories in order to move forward with her life—except on the anniversary of his death. Each year, she'd reflect on the loss and wonder why he'd done it. Margot had said he was bipolar, but in all the time they were together, Catlyn only glimpsed the possibility after he returned from combat.

But after the recent call, she hadn't slept well. The night swirled with dreams that twisted reality into a series of half-truths—troubles that could almost be real, but weren't. Soon, she might be facing a man she'd once loved and lost all those years ago. Or was that eerie voice on the phone only a dream? If it wasn't, was she meeting him at the coffee shop? They wouldn't know each other anymore. She wasn't sure what she expected to find there. What would be the purpose? Closure? Rekindling? Or maybe just the answer to a question that had haunted her for most of her life.

The coffee shop was only a fifteen-minute drive from her house. She'd showered and dressed, as if on autopilot. Now, she stood at the kitchen sink, the coffee untouched in her hand, her eyes fixed on the oak tree outside. The leaves trembled in the wind, like something afraid. The call had come from a number without a caller ID. No name. Just that voice—Jody's voice, aged and distant but unmistakable. The disbelief hadn't faded—if anything; it had increased.

By noon, she might be sitting across from Jody. She could barely remember the contours of his face, only the way it felt to be near him—like holding on to something unstable and electric. They wouldn't recognize each other. Maybe that was the point. Maybe the man who had called her wasn't him. Or maybe he was. She couldn't decide which version of the truth frightened her more.

⌯

Catlyn arrived ten minutes early and chose a seat by the window facing the street. The shop hadn't changed. The same warped wood tables, uneven floor tiles, and chalkboard menu with its exaggerated sideways cursive. Her hands were cold. She ordered tea, though she knew she wouldn't drink it. When the server placed it on the table, she encircled it hoping to find some solace in its warmth.

Time moved in swirls as she waited. The clink of cups, the hiss of the espresso machine, and the murmur of casual conversation formed a backdrop that didn't match her state of mind. She glanced at the door each time it opened, unsure of what she was hoping for. A stranger who would put the past to rest, or something impossible.

Then he walked in. Or someone who looked like him.

The man hesitated at the threshold, scanning the room as if deciding whether he belonged. His hair was salt and pepper grey, trimmed short. His shoulders broader, his face leaner, more worn. He didn't look exactly like the Jody she remembered, but the shape of his hands, the way he adjusted the collar of his coat, the stillness in his expression…struck her like an old chord plucked from nowhere.

He saw her. A flicker of a smile crossed his face. Recognition? Doubt? He walked over to the table.

"Hi," he said, standing there as if waiting for permission to exist.

"Jody?" she asked.

He nodded slowly. "Yes."

They stared at each other for a beat too long. She gestured toward the empty chair.

He sat, folding his hands on the table.

After an interminably long pause, she said, "I thought you were dead."

"I was." His voice carried no irony.

Her heart fluttered. His words sounded like something Jody would say. Something he had said after a combat mission when he was thinner, angrier, and less sure of the world.

"Part of me didn't make it back."

"You left a letter. Margot called me with the horrible news. There was a death notice."

He nodded again, but this time his expression tightened, as if remembering the hurt he'd felt and inflicted.

"I needed to disappear."

She let the words sit between them. Her fingers tightened around her cup. Quietly, she said, "I was devastated."

"I know," he said just as quietly.

"Why now?"

He stared past her out the shop window. "Several months ago, I heard your name. I was at a veteran's event in Boston. Someone mentioned you'd written a book. I started thinking—maybe it was time. Maybe it wasn't too late to say, I'm sorry. Or—to say something."

"You could have sent a letter or reached out years ago." She didn't know what to feel. Anger? Relief? Her body felt unmoored.

He ran his fingers through his hair. "I was afraid you wouldn't read it."

She studied him for a long moment, unsure where the fantasy ended and the truth began. "Where were you all this time?"

He hesitated. "My work…it became something I couldn't talk about. Not to family, to friends, to you—it was classified. I went deeper into it than I had expected. After a while, it became easier— safer—for everyone to think I was gone."

Catlyn blinked hard. "So, *they* faked your death?"

"After what happened with my parents, with you…there wasn't much left to hold me in place."

They fell into silence again, not the kind that asks to be filled, but the kind that settles like dust over years of neglect.

Outside, a bicycle zipped past the window. The moment felt surreal. Like an unattainable blink in time.

Catlyn looked at him intently. The one question she'd wanted to ask for decades came out along with a tear. "Why me, Jody? Why come back to me?"

He looked down, his jaw twitched, and then he met her eyes.

"Because—Catlyn, you were the last person who knew who I was—before I became someone I didn't recognize."

She studied him again. Not the soldier. Not the young man. He had changed, but his voice and the look in his eyes hadn't. When he'd said her name, a flicker of emotions, feelings still remaining, passed between them. For forty years, she had imagined what she'd say. Now, she couldn't remember any of the words. Now that he'd come back, what would come next? Only time would tell.

PART TWO

THE TRAVELING
DETECTIVE

SCIENCE GONE AMISS - 1984

The folder on my desk contained a report from the local precinct. It indicated several days had passed since Doctor Charles Goodman had last been seen. Truth be told, it felt like another bit of nothing our local sheriff had flung my way to keep me off his back. He'd done this often whenever I'd driven over and asked for unsolved cases to investigate. This was the sheriff's usual approach, as he had little regard for private detectives, much less for female sleuths, even though I usually produced results. I decided to stew over the case for an hour or so before following up.

A Mr. Paul Jordan had called the precinct to report that the doctor had been missing for three days, during which time Paul had seen movements and lights ablaze in Goodman's greenhouse at all hours. Because of their long-standing friendship, Goodman and Jordan were neighbors and old friends, who talked daily, so Jordan had been alarmed when the doctor didn't answer his door. The police had driven over to the property and had also knocked on the door with no response. Nothing strange or out of place was seen through the windows. They planned to drive by the house for the next few days and told Mr. Jordan to notify them if he heard from Dr. Goodman in the meantime.

Sipping my tea while looking out into Rock Creek Park and fiddling with my business card, I wondered why I ever became a detective. I had a degree in criminology and, therefore, was qualified, but it was a man's world, and probably always would be. I'd kept my hair cropped short and often dressed in a suit and tie, which made me resemble Annie Hall from the Woody Allen film of the same name. But I didn't fool anyone at the precinct. Initially, I had meant this to be my full-time vocation, but shortly thereafter, I realized this wasn't entirely practical. So, to supplement my income, I'd started a bakery on the street level of a brownstone, purchased with some money I'd borrowed from my father, and lived in the apartment above it. My long-term friend, Terrie Irwin, became my business partner. When we weren't spending hours baking and bulking up our hands from kneading bread in the wee hours, we were solving mysteries. We never managed to get enough sleep.

"Good morning, detective. Got any assignments?" That was Terrie's usual question whenever she appeared in the office. These days, the answer was very often no. She pulled off her baker's hat and apron—still dusted with flour and the warmth of the kitchen—and put them on a hook on the wall in exchange for her "detective cap". A soft wool newsboy style she wore more for ritual than utility. Twisting her hair and piling it under the cap with exaggerated motions was part performance, part shield, and a long-standing joke between us.

About 10:30 a.m. someone knocked on the door. The knock was heavy, impatient, and landed like a demand. Terrie opened the door and was nearly bowled over by a man in his late forties. Someone running on nerves. In that moment, one thought crossed my mind with the kind of solemnity... *The victims are the murdered and the living.*

He wore a rumpled sports jacket, an open shirt, and a pair of blue jeans with a crease ironed down the front. His hair was cropped short, but uncombed.

"Can we help you?" I asked, though I already suspected we would.

"My name is Paul Jordan. Are you Detective Fiona Lynch?" He flicked his hand toward Terrie. "And who is this?"

"Yes. And this is my business partner, Terrie. Would you like some tea?" His nerves were no doubt frazzled as he kept moving his hands—rubbing his neck, twiddling his thumbs, or fidgeting with the buttons on his jacket.

"Tea? Have anything stronger? No, I suppose not. So, yes." He sat down in the armchair.

Terrie fixed some tea using the hot water kettle on top of a cabinet in the corner of the room. I glanced at her and winked when she opened the cabinet door and put two ounces of whiskey into the tea. When she handed it to him, her voice was matter-of-fact.

"Here you go. I added something stronger. We are not above such things."

"Bless you." The first sip tightened his lips. The sun reflected off his face, and it became apparent he had been up all night. His eyes were puffy and bloodshot. After a few swallows of the concoction, he began to speak, haltingly at first. He relayed the same story he'd told the police. The lights. The silence. The sense that something had shifted from odd to ominous. The police had shrugged it all off.

Finally, he said, "I suspect something terrible has happened to the doctor, but I have no way of proving anything. The police don't seem at all concerned about the situation. I came across someone you had helped in the past, and they said you could probably solve this mystery."

"We will do our best. But first, we'll need to start at the beginning." I rubbed my chin. It had become a bothersome habit. "What is his profession?"

"Yes, al'right. Charles is a damn good researcher. He's authored over a hundred publications, won awards, and patented various works. His current project has to do with a cure for immune deficiencies."

Terrie leaned forward. "Mr. Jordan, when and where did you last see him?"

"Please, call me Paul." He squeezed his knee before continuing. "Four nights ago. We were both returning from work at about six o'clock. We meet regularly at the mailbox at the end of the driveway. He was unusually talkative and excited. Said something big had happened."

Paul went on—sometimes focused, sometimes scattered—shifting between facts and memories with no clear boundary between the two. He seemed, understandably, unable to keep track of all our questions.

"Hold on." I gently interrupted his monologue to take a moment to process everything and add to my notes. "Let me catch up. All right. Now, tell me what he looks like."

Paul blinked hard. "My age. Late forties. Five-feet tall, brown eyes, black hair, a mustache—and slender. That night he was wearing a shirt and tie, slacks, and his white lab coat. Oh, and he had his briefcase. He was so worked up; he forgot to take his lab coat off before he left work. We parted, and I haven't seen him since."

"So, this wasn't his usual behavior?" Terrie said from her perch in the corner.

"You're not listening," he snapped.

"I certainly am. Just clarifying," Terrie replied with a steady voice.

He deflated. "I'm sorry. I'm not usually this rude. Forgive me."

"Yes, well," I interjected. "Stress of this kind can bring out all kinds of..." I was interrupted before I could finish.

"I suppose." He sighed audibly. "That night, I couldn't stay asleep and was roaming around the house at midnight. Out my kitchen window, I noticed the greenhouse lights were on. Charles was pacing and waving his hands around like he was arguing with himself. I've seen him do that before, but this ...this was different."

"So, you have a good view. Is it your custom to look in people's windows at night?" Terrie asked, her tone somewhere between dry and amused.

"Not usually. I couldn't avoid seeing. The greenhouse lights were bright, and they've never been on at night before. We are on one-acre lots with some trees between us, but the houses are only about one-hundred feet apart."

"And after that?" I encouraged him on.

"Every night, same thing. During the day—nothing. No sign of him. I phoned multiple times, but he never answered. The lights came on for several nights."

"Anyone else in the area?" Terrie asked.

Paul shook his head. "Charles has been a research scientist at Sloan University for the past ten years. He's spent the last five years trying to find the cure for a deadly disease. We all know it very well at this point—AIDS. He was primarily getting his funding from the local Pathology Foundation, as well as lab space from the university. The last time we talked, he told me in quite a hush-hush manner that he'd discovered the cure but needed to conduct some trials on humans. He had arranged to have a meeting with his supporters at the foundation four days after that evening, which was yesterday. I suspect he didn't show."

Paul handed us cards with the foundation's address and the name of the person to contact; Ms. Jean Monroe. I told him we'd begin investigating within the next few hours. He thanked us, scribbled out a check with a trembling hand, and placed it on my desk. The amount exceeded our usual fees.

"I'll be at home," he said on his way out the door, "trying to sleep."

༄

I wrote down additional thoughts while they were fresh in my mind. Terrie looked on with her hands folded across her yellow notepad.

Soon enough, she would input whatever was said, along with her own thoughts, into the computer.

"Terrie, what do you think? Do we have enough for a case?" I asked.

"I'm not sure. The doctor could just be in some sort of self-imposed seclusion until he completes the final stages of his research." Terrie picked up her pencil and scribbled something on her notepad.

"Perhaps, but I think there is more here than there appears. I agree with Paul. I think there has been some foul play." It was time for me to consider having a whiskey without tea. "The first question I asked myself—does Paul have any motives for creating such a story? I don't think so. And where is the doctor? I've two ideas. First, I'll contact Ms. Monroe at the foundation and see what kind of setup they have there. See if I can get you inside for a few days, so you can thoroughly investigate. If my theory is correct, the entire mystery can be solved within their walls."

"And I can check things out at the university. I understand there is a lot of competition among professors to get their new ideas published. And they 'spy' on each other."

"Well, al'right, that makes some sense." It was my turn to make some more notations on my own notepad. "I imagine the university only provides the doctor with workspace, and from the conversation we had with Paul, they haven't been told about the doctor's latest discoveries. Just to play it safe, I'll call ahead before going over there. Maybe they know where Dr. Goodman is. If not, they'll surely know about his research. Afterwards, we can regroup here and go visit his house."

"Sounds good." Terrie stood up, grabbed her apron from a hook on the way, and tied it securely around her waist before exchanging her cap with her chef's hat. "I'll go back down to the bakery. I didn't quite finish everything this morning. I suspect Kate needs a break. Business has picked up, and the ovens are constantly running."

I drove up the long winding driveway of the foundation in my old, green four-door sedan. The campus stretched over two acres of land, dotted with trees, both old and recently planted on the immaculate grounds. The building itself was surrounded by vibrant azalea bushes. It looked more like a home than a business.

The main building was freshly painted in white, with black shutters, and a three-story high porch. A U-shaped driveway curved in front of a house. To the right of the building, the doors on a car barn were wide open. I counted six stalls, two of them filled with classic cars—a Bentley and a Mercedes. Perhaps it was a carriage house at some point. Details can be important as a case evolves. Another driveway extended from the car barn to a modest sized visitors' parking area—about six spaces.

When I entered the building, I was greeted by Ms. Monroe at the reception desk. As we toured the facility, I took detailed notes on a legal pad, which Terrie would add to the case file in the afternoon.

It is funny, when I think back to our first case, it seemed foolish to record everything in minutiae, but I had learned from experience that the details often come in handy. In the Pathology Foundation, there was a comfortable dining area on one side and a living room on the other, both with available partitions to allow for private gatherings. The rooms directly behind them had long tables with plenty of seating for meetings. Behind these rooms, there was an expansive kitchen with all the amenities for full course meals. At the rear of the building, near the kitchen, was an old-fashioned elevator with a wrought-iron gate.

In the middle of the space, an oak staircase led to the offices. They were quite different from the first floor as they were decorated quite similarly to any other office one might imagine. Everyone except the two secretaries had their own offices around the outer walls. At the top of the stairs, on the wall directly opposite, was a large picture window with secretaries' desks on either side. On the remaining three sides of the stairs, there were seven rooms with closed doors. According to the secretary, who greeted me at the top of the stairs, the attic was filled with boxes full of documents. I wasn't sure why she was compelled to impart this information. As for me, I considered large quantities of paper in attics a fire hazard. Perhaps the walls had been insulated and enclosed. I needed to examine all the related documents to determine if anyone at the foundation had access to the specifics of Dr. Goodman's research.

"Ms. Monroe, I believe what I'm working on is extremely sensitive. Is there a place we can meet privately?"

We went into her office. I shut the door behind me before she had a chance to say anything.

"Now, tell me what kind of situation we are dealing with. What I can do to help?" Ms. Monroe asked.

"When was the last time you heard from Dr. Goodman?"

"About five days ago. We arranged to meet in my office, but he didn't show up."

"Did he tell you anything about his findings?"

"No, he just said he'd come up with something 'brilliant', and I needed to hear about it firsthand. He said, we'd be famous soon."

"Ms. Monroe, do you think there is any possibility of foul play? I imagine there are many people who'd love to reap the benefits of any discoveries."

"That never crossed my mind."

"Well, what do you suppose could have happened to him?"

"I—I really can't imagine. I hope he is safe somewhere. I really don't want to think anyone here would actually do anything awful to him."

"Where does he keep his research papers?"

"They would be either at the university lab or at his house."

"My assistant, Terrie, and I will go to his place later this afternoon. Has there been any unusual activity at the foundation in the past ten days or so that you're aware of?"

"Well, yes. Six months ago, I leased the adjacent building that used to be the servants' quarters more than a hundred years ago, to a middle-aged couple named Mr. and Mrs. James Lacey. In the past few weeks, there have been a lot of people entering and exiting the building with brown packages. I haven't reported it to the police because I didn't feel there was anything illegal going on."

"Does your receptionist keep any kind of records of people coming into the foundation? And can you give me a list of the individuals involved with any other research you fund?"

"Yes, I can get them right away, but you'll have to wait half an hour while I get the receptionist to make a copy of her log. We have always kept careful records. I will say I'm looking forward to getting our files on the newfangled computers, but I don't entirely trust them yet."

"Al'right, I will wait for the information. In the meantime, I have one additional special request."

"Of course."

"I strongly believe he's either been kidnapped or murdered."

"Murdered," she said in a low, quavering voice.

"Yes, murdered. I can't explain yet, but if his research is as important as you say, I think he could very well be dead. I sincerely hope I'm wrong. The lights his neighbor saw at night could be a person trying to locate his research papers. I need you to allow me to do two things. One, let my business partner pose as your assistant, and allow me to come in as a visiting editor. I didn't tell the receptionist why I came here today beyond asking to see you, so she shouldn't be confused. I will need a private space to work, with a window, preferably with a view of your tenant's lodgings."

"You can have full rein of the place if it will help you discover the doctor's whereabouts."

"I must ask you to keep our discussion strictly confidential and find logical ways to explain our presence to your staff. Do you have anything my assistant can do?

"Yes, absolutely. The boxes in the attic need to be reorganized. It will take months to get everything into our computers. She can spend the day up there weeding through the documents."

"Good, thank you." After I received the lists I needed, I popped into the car and skimmed through them.

❧

When I arrived back at the office, Terrie had finished in the bakery and was working at the computer.

"Did you get anywhere with Ms. Monroe?" Terrie asked.

"I went over a list of names on a printout she provided noting the people who were in the office last month. She also gave me the names of the researchers who might take an interest in Dr. Goodman's findings."

"Great," Terrie said.

"Before we start analyzing the lists, what did you learn at the university?" I asked.

"The administrative office told me where to locate the doctor's student assistant. I phoned her, and she met me at the office."

"Good."

"Her name is Beth. She told me she hadn't been to Dr. Goodman's lab in a week. I asked her why. She said he'd told her he was nearly at the end of his research and needed some time alone. She didn't mind, as her main duty of late had been purchasing various chemicals on his behalf. Otherwise, he was a fairly self-sufficient man. Since we were near the lab, it seemed as good a time as any to investigate. Beth handed me the keys. She was babbling nonsense when she saw the state of things. The place was in shambles. Papers were scattered all over the floor, but the cabinets full of chemicals and supplies were untouched. The cages, which I assumed were for experimental animals, were all empty. That confused me then and still does. I called the precinct, and they agreed to send over a team to sweep the place for relevant evidence. The chief isn't turning a blind eye anymore. As for Beth, I can't imagine any reason she'd want to get rid of the doctor."

"Good God—you should have told me about the lab the second you found out." I tried to hold my temper. Instead of reading her the riot act, I growled and grabbed my bag filled with investigative gadgets. "No one is above suspicion at this point. I think we should go to his house right away to see if anything else is amiss."

∽

We didn't waste any time driving over to the doctor's house. As Paul said, his place was not far away. Both of their houses were buffered from the main road by bushes, making it fairly easy for anyone to move around the property undetected from the street. We approached cautiously, knocked on the heavy oak door, and waited. After several attempts, no one answered.

"Terrie, before we go any further, run next door and get Paul. If there is anything we're missing, he'll spot it more easily than we can. Remember to watch his every move. We want to make sure he's not a suspect. While you're gone, I will look around the outside of this place."

Terrie returned with Paul. I hadn't discovered anything unusual in that brief span of time. We all put on thin latex gloves that I kept in my bag to avoid disturbing any fingerprints in case this turned into a criminal investigation.

I inserted the key and opened the door slowly to find an oriental rug in the foyer folded over on itself. The overall decor of the house had a Victorian feel, with dark-wood furnishings. We began to walk through the place. I put my hand up to stop the others for a moment, and put a finger to my lips to tell Paul not to speak, and then motioned them to continue to follow me. I needed to assess the situation before starting a conversation. I looked closer at the foyer, pushing the rug further back, and noticed fresh scuff marks. Moving left towards the kitchen, I saw that most of the cabinets and drawers were open. Passing through an archway, we found nothing scattered about in either the dining or living room. Further into the house, in the bedroom, there were a few clothes thrown on an unmade bed, but the rest of the room was orderly with books piled neatly on a dresser. The closet was full of clothing and shoes. The rooms smelled faintly of men's cologne.

Across from the living room, I saw the entrance to the greenhouse and put my bag down by the door. As soon as I opened it, a gray cat came bounding out with a cry of apparent objection to being left alone for way too long. It rubbed against all of our ankles before glaring at the empty food bowl by the door. Just beyond him, there were reddish-brown cat footprints on the tiles. I scooped him up and examined his paws, but found nothing unusual. For precautionary purposes, I closed the door to the house so the cat wouldn't leave. I further enticed him with a few kibbles in his food bowl from a plastic bin, but there wasn't enough for a full meal.

The greenhouse was impressive, with all kinds of plants, shrubs, and a few trees. Some of the plants had been knocked over; some larger pots were missing, which was evident from the dirt rings on the floor.

In the center of the room was a twelve-foot-long framed table filled with several inches of dirt. The cat's reddish-brown footprints led up to it. In one a corner a small hole had been dug, undoubtedly, by the cat. I stuck my gloved hand in the dirt and turned over the soil, expecting to find cat droppings, but the soil wasn't the right color. I retrieved my benzidine spray and a trowel from my bag in the hall. I applied it to the surface.

"Blood," I said, "but without testing it, I can't say if it's animal or human."

Paul's face turned ghostly white. I thought he might faint, but he stood steady. Our enforced silence momentarily broke in a collective gasp.

Without further delay, I pulled a plastic bag out of my pocket and collected a sample with a trowel for testing. The dirt mixture I collected was a darker color than the rest, but was dry enough not to get attached to the trowel. Behind the long table, a small refrigerator was mounted on the wall, and next to it was a much smaller table with a lone wooden box. I lifted the box upward, and it came away from its base. Inside I found a microscope with slides and associated paraphernalia. Then, I opened the refrigerator and found blood samples in test tubes. It seemed strange that the doctor would have these around his home instead of keeping them at the lab. Without further delay, I motioned to the others to follow me outside. On the way, I scooped up the cat. He would be better off in my apartment for the time being.

We walked to the end of the driveway in silence. Paul's face was still unnaturally pale. I broke the hush looming over us.

"Paul, I realize you are upset, but I want you to go home and tell no one of our findings. I'll get the dirt tested."

"Be assured we'll do all we can." Terrie added, resting her hand on his arm.

I continued. "While I wait for the test results, we'll go ahead with the investigation. If the doctor appears, please tell him not to worry about—let me see…" I examined the cat's collar as it peered up at me with saucer-sized eyes. "Smitty."

☙

By the time we'd dropped off the dirt sample at the forensic lab and picked up some things at the pet store, an hour had passed. Terrie set up the cat paraphernalia in the bathroom while I made some tea and grabbed a sandwich from the bakery. We didn't usually sell them, but we had plenty of meat and cheese in the fridge for our own purposes. Maybe we'd put more than bread permanently on the menu at some point, but we hadn't gotten around to it yet.

We went upstairs to the office and began reviewing our suspects and our next move.

"First, we have Paul Jordan. Terrie, would you agree he isn't involved other than reporting his suspicions?"

"Yes, from the look on his face when we discovered the blood and his general behavior, I would rule him out."

"Then there are the Laceys, who rent the house next to the foundation, but we know next to nothing about them other than the excessive number of couriers coming to their home."

"We have Gloria, the receptionist. And random staff members." Terrie continued. "None of the others, except the researchers, seem to have anything to gain from getting Dr. Goodman out of the way. After all, Ms. Monroe did say the person who came up with the cure, along with the foundation, would not only be rich but famous."

The phone rang. It was my friend Sam with the results of the soil analysis. The blood was human; B-positive. I thanked him and hung up.

"Terrie, we have work to do. We need to find a body. Sam is sending a messenger over with a new gadget. When it arrives, we'll go back to his home and search the grounds for clues."

"Yes, Ma'am."

"With the amount of blood, assuming it is Dr. Goodman's, he couldn't have walked out of the greenhouse. There should be drag marks we missed on the first visit."

We spent a good portion of the day combing the ground for any signs of disturbance. We found a few meaningless trinkets and a gold watch engraved with the Goodman's name.

Terrie and I went into the greenhouse. I waved the detector over every plant and table. There was nothing more. Then I looked in every corner and crevice in the place. An hour later, I found a neatly folded set of clothes behind a partition. They were the same ones

Mr. Jordan had described: a pair of tan slacks, a red shirt, a white tie, and a pair of loafers. Behind a partition, a white lab jacket and a pair of underpants hung over a folded chair.

My mind was racing. Where was the doctor? This case had me rattled, because this missing man could be the key to a major medical discovery. Was the he hiding out somewhere? Or had he been kidnapped or murdered? All viable possibilities. I wandered around the building until I found a phone, donned a pair of gloves to keep my fingerprints off the receiver, and called the police precinct and the forensics lab. Both said they'd notify me if anyone who resembled him was brought into the morgue.

Back outside, I found Terrie sitting on the steps and showed her what I'd found. "We have a bunch of names, clothes, human blood in the dirt, and a motive."

"Don't forget, Paul said the doctor had a briefcase the last time they met. We didn't find it anywhere. If it contained the final results of his AIDS research, it was probably stolen."

"I feel the chances are pretty good. The police will be on the lookout tonight. Let's get some sleep and start fresh in the morning at the foundation offices. Remember, we don't know each other when we're there."

"Right. We'll spend the day blending in. Hopefully, we'll find some clues."

"Terrie, before you go home for the evening, return the keys to his assistant."

"Her name was—Beth? I must be tired not to have recalled it right away."

"Thank you. While you are there, ask her to go through his papers to see if there's anything left of his research or curative formulas."

"I don't think there will be anything. Someone else wants the credit."

"And financial rewards. We'll go through this process anyway. I'll be at the Foundation around ten tomorrow. In the meantime, privately ask Beth if there are any new developments. When I arrive at the offices, nod at me if there are any. I will ask for Ms. Monroe. It's important that you don't treat me like someone you know. Remember our cover."

"Right, I've done this show with you before." Terrie guffawed.

"You're from Friday Temp Agency. I called them and they put you in their records. You're filling in for Gloria at the front desk while she does some other work. Begin a thorough study of the receptionist's work and make a copy of anything suspicious. Unless an emergency arises, let's plan to meet in our office tomorrow night."

∽

Terrie arrived at the foundation around 8:30 a.m. the next morning and settled herself in for a long day. She observed everyone who came into the office and made a special effort to be friendly, as she didn't know who might give her a lead to the doctor's whereabouts. She wrote down who everyone was and why they were there, whether they were there all day or passing through. Fortunately, this was company policy and would not bring her presence to anyone's attention. Terrie took the information home with her and entered it into her private records while she ate a Hungryman™ frozen dinner at her kitchen table. She also loaded the information from the disc onto her private computer to study. She had considered printing everything, but having pieces of paper scattered about was no longer an option she preferred. Those days were gone.

∽

When I went into the foundation offices at 10 a.m., Terrie signaled nothing had been discovered.

"Good morning," Ms. Monroe said. "Are you ready to get to work on editing?

"Yes, ma'am," I replied.

We walked down the hall and into Ms. Monroe's office. She promptly closed the door. "I have collected some background information on the people you checked off on the list yesterday. Is there a way we can narrow the list down together?"

"Yes, I should think so," I replied. "Ms. Monroe, we appreciate your cooperation. The evidence is leading more and more toward murder. All the research seems to have vanished. We have two problems; we don't have any viable suspects, and we haven't found a body."

"To make things worse, if that's possible," Ms. Monroe said, "there is no cure for AIDS. The press hasn't got a hold of his conclusions or his absence, so that's one less thing to worry about."

"We have to find a way to flush the culprit out before they cover their tracks further or leave the country," I said.

"The motive is so obvious. I'm sure the person would not be foolish enough to stick around unless—unless they thought they'd gotten away with the crime." Ms. Monroe threw up her hands.

"Yes, another reason to keep this investigation as secret as possible. We have to help the thief or thieves believe they got away with it. Whoever they are may come forward with the cure, claiming to have no knowledge of anyone else's research. By then, I hope to have found enough evidence against them. I imagine the person will wait a while to come forward."

"I can save you some time. Upon further consideration, the only other person who could come forward without raising suspicion is Dr. Abramson. Let me explain. He, too, had been given a grant to do AIDS research about seven years ago. He has been working diligently since then. They took different paths with their research. Eventually, Dr. Abramson's grant money was decreased at the Board of Director's discretion."

"Have the members met?"

"Not officially. If they met unofficially, I would have no idea." Ms. Monroe stood up and paced between her desk and the window.

"Last month, Dr. Abramson told the board members he had found a cure. Next week, we have an appointment in my office to turn in the results. Dr. Goodman made an appointment to do the very same thing, but his appointment has come and gone."

∽

I'm in the bakery kneading bread way too early in the morning. So far, there haven't been any new findings since Terrie and I spent a day at the foundation with our ears and eyes open. The renters next door to the foundation are no longer receiving packages, according to Ms. Monroe. Paul has not reported seeing anyone at the doctor's house. My mind is turning over all the facts. I keep coming back to the neighbors. Why are they renting the small house next to the foundation? They are not faculty. They are not students. No one has talked to them about the case as far as I know. Could they be involved? I need to talk to them while Terrie waits in the car.

I went over and knocked on the door. A woman with a tight gray bun on the top of her head answered the door. She was stiff and lean, with walrus-like wrinkles on her face, neck, and arms. When we shook hands, I noticed the skin on her hands was as thin as tissue paper with prominent blue veins running towards polished violet nails. She had little to say, but before I could question her beyond a civil hello and providing my title, a man with a similar appearance came up behind her to interrupt our conversation. His gray hair was loose on his shoulders. The texture of his face and hands were similar to the woman's.

"How may I help you?" The man said in an accent I couldn't decipher.

"Hello, I'm Detective Lynch." I took the soft route and smiled while showing my identification. "I'm investigating the whereabouts of a missing person. Perhaps you could help?"

"I hope I can be of assistance," the man said, and stepped back a few steps into the foyer. "Come in."

"I understand from a Ms. Monroe that you and your wife only recently moved in?"

"True, but this is not my wife. Dahlia rented the place." The man hesitated. "I am a guest. My name is Claus Abramson."

Could this be the Dr. Abramson? Instead, I said, "I'm looking for a person connected with the foundation next door, and hoped you might have seen him. Dr. Goodman?"

Abramson laughed. "He is not missing. Come with me."

With reservations, I followed him up the stairs, with Dahlia close behind me. Down a corridor, we entered a room full of light and a maze of topiaries. In a carved-out section, shaped like a horseshoe, I saw the back of a hospital bed. Next to it, several bags of liquid were hanging off an IV stand.

"Come, come," Dahlia said. "Meet Dr. Goodman."

Right then, I knew my investigation was over. I introduced myself and apologized for the intrusion. "You've been missed by your neighbor, Paul. He thought you'd been kidnapped or murdered. Your cat's not too happy either. He made bloody paw prints in your greenhouse."

"I'm sorry about my cat. I spilled a test tube of blood in the dirt before I left and didn't bother to clean it up. Don't worry, it's healthy blood." The doctor didn't seem upset in the slightest as a wane smile emerged. He continued. "It was nice of Paul to notice my absence, but as you see, I am right here. You look concerned. I will explain. Through my research, I believe I have found a cure for AIDS, but I am testing it out before submitting my findings to the Board of Directors at the foundation."

"They expected you at a meeting and you never showed," I said.

"My current situation took my mind away from such things. Don't let my looks deceive you. I appear healthy at this point in the disease, but my bloodwork shows otherwise."

"How..."

"The *how* is not important or anyone's business. However, the cure is. If I don't start losing weight or losing my hair, and my skin remains unblemished, there is a good chance this IV drip is working. We will know soon. Nurse Dahlia is testing my blood daily to record my progress."

"Quite a risk you're taking for the advancement of science."

"A luxury I have as a doctor, even though this may be considered unethical. I'm dying if I don't. If this doesn't work, I'll go back to my lab and try again until I'm dead. If it works, I'll face the legal consequences of my current actions."

"Nurse Dahlia and I will too," said Dr. Abramson. "In our defense, millions of lives will be saved."

"Good point," I conceded. "Well, I guess we are done here. Case closed."

THE ROSES - A NEW ERA, 2010

Here I am, Detective Fiona Lynch, back at work in England by chance or fate during my international travels. I'd landed in England for an extended holiday at a family member's home and found myself drawn to mysteries in the news, piecing together the answers before the official reports came out. I reestablished my Interpol connections and was on call at a local office in Nottingham. Terrie, my longtime confidant, often joked that I could never retire, no matter how hard I tried. She wasn't wrong.

I brushed the raindrops off my wool coat and pulled the hood tighter around my thick neck, while cursing the extra pounds I'd picked up over the years. Even my hands had become plump—a far cry from the long-gone slender version of myself. Thirty-plus years had slipped by since then, and the mirror didn't let me forget. From a distance, I figured strangers might mistake me for a man. Maybe a male detective got more respect. That might've been true in the 80s when I started out, but things had changed, if only slightly. The years had worn me thin in all the wrong ways and left me with a hitch in my left hip from arthritis. Most days, there were bigger problems to worry about.

Thirty minutes had gone by since I'd received a phone call and made my way across town to the pub as the sun tried to peek through the clouds.

Passing by the statue of Robin Hood in Nottingham brought a wry smile to my lips. I'd never much liked the piece. To me, it sent the wrong message to the community—redistribution of wealth by

103

any means. The idea was a bit repugnant. The copper cast statue had been hauled to the small park in 1952 and serenaded by a band from the Royal Lincolnshire Regiment at its dedication. *Ah, my England, my England.* I couldn't help thinking about my favorite author, D.H. Lawrence, a momentary distraction before the inevitable confrontation with death.

But today, my concerns about my appearance and local artifacts took a back seat to the case at hand. This wasn't my first time dealing with murder at a pub. Memories of a similar case, one involving a poisoned pint and a love triangle gone wrong, briefly came to mind. That case had been messy, full of twists and turns, and had left me with a deep sense of distrust of ordinary settings. Would this case be as complicated? I'd know soon enough.

As I walked along, I couldn't help being distracted by the latest community project. All over town, there were synthetic robin birds with pointed caps covering their crests mounted in plain sight. It felt like something out of a cheap tourist brochure rather than a homage to history. There were thirty-odd birds, five-meters tall with multiple patchwork colors painted across every inch. They would only remain in place for a mere twelve weeks, then be collected and auctioned off in October. I wondered what the locals really felt about the birds, even though the residents were likely too busy with their daily lives to give them much thought. The money would go to Nottinghamshire Hospice; a good cause I couldn't fault. But still, I found them gaudy.

A few more paces and I'd be at the pub. The name of the place, Ye Olde Trip to Jerusalem Inn, never made much sense to me. Yet, I couldn't argue with anyone on that subject either. After all, the establishment opened in 1189, and I enjoyed going there for a pint of ale. The various rooms were cozy, partially embedded in the rocks at the rear, and each steeped in its own unique charm.

Passing through the stone-lined courtyard into the building brought a familiar mix of emotions. The smell of aged wood, spilled beer, and faint traces of long-extinguished smoke hit me immediately. This pub had seen countless lives pass through its doors, each leaving behind a trace of their story. How many secrets had its walls overheard? And now, it was the scene of another tragedy.

At the bar, I discovered the young woman who'd called the precinct. Her nametag gave her away. Liz was sitting on a stool, downing what appeared to be her second pint. I hoped she hadn't touched anything at the scene beyond the phone and the glass. She gripped it so tightly that I worried it might shatter into pieces.

"Morning, my dear, I was sent by the local DCI. Name's Detective Lynch. Tell me, what happened here?"

"Oh, hiya. I remember you. Seen you in here a few times." Liz responded in an accent that sounded British, but a little American, too.

"That's right, love."

"Sorry, what's a DCI again?"

"Detective Chief Inspector. Like me, you're not from these parts, are you? I hear a hint of something else in your voice."

Liz loosened her grip on the glass, and her hand twitched. "Yes, I'm from the States, but I've been here long enough to work on the accent. I like to blend in. When I found my manager—Mrs. O'Connell—I didn't waste a minute and rang the police. She's over there in the back room by the well. It's quite deep and gloomy to look down into the spider's webs. The water is stagnant, I think, and covered in a thin coat of dust. It smells a bit musty in that room." Liz pointed with a trembling finger, then wiped it on her muslin peasant blouse. I knew from previous visits that everyone was provided with a blouse and either a roughshod pair of trousers or a long skirt to adhere to a medieval ambiance.

"Right then, I'll go have a look. Liz, I'm sure finding your boss like this must have been horrible."

"Yeah, just a shock, I guess. She was always kind to me, you know. Tough, but fair. I can't believe this happened."

I pressed on. "Did Mrs. O'Connell have any conflicts with staff or clients recently?"

The old well was framed by a wrought iron rail to prevent guests from stumbling into the opening, which was haphazardly covered with a piece of Plexiglas. The overwhelming stench of damp and death filled the air. A woman lay prostrate on the floor with a gash across her head. One arm stretched forward with her palm splayed wide open. A line of blood trickled away from her head on the uneven floor.

"Tsk-tsk." I muttered, pulling a digital camera from my coat and began taking photographs. The forensic team would take more photos when they arrived and go over every inch of the pub. There probably weren't any usable fingerprints due to the public nature of the place. Yet, there was one thing unusual lying just beyond Mrs. O'Connell's reach.

"Ma'am," Liz's weak voice emerged.

I crouched near the body, cursing my arthritis while noting a faint imprint of her hand on the dusty floor.

"What—what are those roses? Is Mrs. O'Connell reaching for them?"

I turned my gaze to the bouquet of roses just out of reach. "Appears so." Seven roses, their petals a deep crimson, almost blending with the blood on the floor. The sight sent a chill down my spine. There was something deliberately ritualistic about it. Cases from my past flickered in my mind. I was fairly certain I knew exactly who had murdered Mrs. O'Connell.

"Who could do such a thing?" Liz asked, her voice trembling.

"It wouldn't be prudent to say yet. The information could put you in danger. The apron strings wrapped around the roses are odd." I felt something bite my cheek. "Might be coincidental or could mean something important."

"Not knowing who might have done this will make me more nervous."

"Perhaps, but I still can't tell you. Not until the forensic work is carried out." I felt a welt on my cheek. I don't know why I fussed with it, but I felt like it was getting larger by the second.

"You all right? Your face is getting red."

"Yeah, yeah. Just a bug bite. A cold rag would help." I needed her to leave me alone to think. While she hurried off, I popped an allergy tablet into my mouth. The last time I'd seen a dead body with roses was eighteen months ago. It hadn't been publicized because the old woman's family wanted to keep things quiet. Her death had been deemed an accident, but now… now I wasn't so sure. The current tragedy wasn't going to be kept under wraps. Since Nottingham murders were rare, the press would get a hold of this case.

Liz returned with the rag and handed it to me.

"Liz, do you have a lot of shifts here?" I asked, pressing the cool cloth to my cheek.

"Mostly on weekends," Liz replied. "I'm at Uni during the week."

"Were there any regular customers on your shifts?"

"Yeah, sure. There was this one bloke last week who got into a row with Mrs. O'Connell over his tab. He's always loud when he's had too much to drink. I didn't think it was anything serious."

"If I describe one of them, would you recognize him?"

"Description? Not likely. But a photo, probably. No need, really. There's a surveillance camera in the corner. You know, a CCTV? Trouble is, it's only aimed at the bar, not the well."

"Can you show me?"

"Yeah, no worries. My brother taught me. He works at a security firm back home."

"Very good. Let's have a look." I followed Liz into a back room that was more of a closet. After making a quick decision, I decided not to divulge anything. I didn't want to put her life in danger, too. "Liz, show me the footage from last night. About an hour before closing. Point out anyone you recognize as a regular."

"Yeah, all right." She clicked the computer mouse here and there as I looked on. "Nothing was stolen. I checked. And there aren't any treasures of Grantham in the caves below us to steal."

She pointed to him and six other gents. The pieces began to fall into place. It didn't take long before I saw the man who was the most likely culprit. The accidental death of an old woman, Mrs. Crump, came to mind. Her death had been called an accident, but now I was pretty sure it couldn't have been. She'd died at home clutching a bouquet of seven roses. The official report concluded she'd fallen down the stairs, but now, seeing this scene, I wasn't so sure. Jerald, Mrs. Crump's son, had been at home the night his mother died. And here he was—caught on the CCTV, swaying drunkenly on a barstool. It might be a coincidental connection, but I had probable cause to revisit the 'accidental' death.

"Liz, put a sign out front on the far side of the courtyard saying; *Sorry, closed until tomorrow.*' We can't have people mucking about. You can go on home when you're done."

"Yeah, al'right. No Sunday Roast—the clients aren't going to like that." She scurried off to find paper, pen, and string to tie her sign onto the notice board outside, then disappeared out the door.

The forensic team appeared. I briefed them quickly, showed them my photos, and left them to their work. My next stop was Jerald Crump's residence. With any luck, the man would be home at this hour, sleeping off his stupor. Using my phone, I searched the database for Jerald's address and called in for backup. Half an hour later, I knocked on the door while two officers stood off to the side.

At first there was no response, but then a disheveled, dark-haired man opened the door. Jerald Crump. He blinked at me, startled, and backed up a step, colliding with a woman who had been standing behind him.

I explained the scene at the pub and compared it to Jerald's mother's prostrate body with the bouquet of roses. Jerald's face grew red with agitation. He claimed he didn't recall being at the pub the night before. "I was home all night," he insisted. "I don't even like the place. And my poor mum…I can't believe you'd drag her into this! She was ill—dementia had her so confused and angry all the time."

His denials were convincing, but I wasn't particularly sympathetic. I signaled for the officer to take Jerald into custody for questioning. As he was led out, the woman, who had been standing quietly behind him, grabbed her coat to follow. As she moved, something fell from her pocket—a handful of rose petals.

I bent to pick them up, my mind racing. The woman looked at me, her expression suddenly guarded.

"Care to explain these?" I asked, holding a petal between my fingers.

Her lips pressed into a thin line. She didn't answer.

Gesturing to the officers, I said, "Take her in as well. Your boss can sort this mess out at the station."

The roses, the deaths, the strange connections—all of it would need unraveling. But for now, we had two suspects and a growing sense that the case was far from over.

PART THREE

HEIDI AND
FAMILY

LEFT BEHIND

Rita, after becoming a WWII widow, kept her first-born child, whose name was Mina. Some time later, she met another soldier and became pregnant out of wedlock, but that man vanished without a trace. Mina found out about the lost baby when she was six years old, although she never knew why her mother told her. Up until that point, Mina's life had been difficult, and it did not get better after learning she had a younger sister who had escaped her fate.

Rita tried to find out what had happened to her second baby's father. She wrote to the Army asking them to provide his address or forward her letter. When the Army's return letter arrived, she ripped it open. They didn't respond in a way she could dispute. The powers that be declared they could only forward letters or give addresses to the immediate family members. Since she had not married the baby's father, the Army was not obligated to help her in any way.

Was he dead, too? Had he forgotten her? Rita thought he must be dead since she was sure he would have come back. He knew where she was. She considered traveling to his hometown to search on her own, but the city was far away and too big for her to have any chance of success.

The baby was given up for adoption the day she was born.

After regaining her strength, Rita returned to her two jobs while her mother tended to her firstborn. Working at the grocery store was never quite the same, but making ice cream for parlors—*Eis Dieles*—helped her hold on to her husband's memory. After all, they had met over ice cream. To get her mind off the decision she'd felt forced to make, Rita hoped to either reunite with her second baby or determine if the Catholic nuns had found her a new home.

The months crept by. Nothing in her life was working out the way she'd hoped. Her friends didn't understand or know how to help, and many of them had abandoned her over the last two years. She had become somewhat of an outcast. They all knew her husband was dead and couldn't have been the father of the baby she gave up for adoption. Her friends labeled her a pariah, an undesirable woman, who would never find a respectable husband.

Rita scooped up Mina, and they took the thirty-minute bus ride to the convent. She hoped the presence of her older daughter would soften the nun's resolve. She watched Mina peer happily through the window while the scenery sped by. Today, the world was full of possibilities for her daughter. But for Rita, there was only sorrow.

Rita's eyes teared up on a regular basis, and today was no different. Why? Why did all these things have to happen? When would life become less turbulent?

The nuns were surprisingly kind and said Mina was old enough to have supervised playtime with a few of the orphans while the adults talked.

"Go on," Rita said. "Go with the nun. I'll come collect you, don't worry." Rita nudged Mina toward the nun in the hallway. The woman took her hand and escorted her away with another child.

Rita went into the Reverend Mother's office and sat in the same chair she had sat in when she'd given up her baby. The Reverend Mother said her baby had been adopted quickly. Her hopes of having a glimpse were gone in a flash.

"Who has my baby? Is she well cared for?" Followed by, "What's her name, and where is she?"

"Remember, you relinquished your rights to such information," the Reverend Mother said. "The child's new parents are living in Paris. I can't tell you anything else."

Rita stared into the fireplace behind the nun and watched while the white smoke rose like a spirit, carrying her last hope with it.

"I'm sorry your life has been difficult, but know you are not alone. The Lord has not abandoned you. Your baby is in good hands and will never want for anything."

"I understand, but I'm sad all the time."

"*Konzentriere dich auf die Tocher, die du behalten hast* (stay focused on the daughter you kept). The nun said this with a stoic, flat voice.

"Thank you for your help." Rita couldn't think of anything else to say.

"Excuse me, I must get back to my duties. Sister Mary will take you to Mina."

Rita followed the nun into the recreation hall, where Mina was happily playing and chattering away with the other children. She lifted Mina into her arms as her daughter kicked and screamed in protest. Rita wanted to scream too—but adults weren't supposed to do such things within the sacred halls. But then she realized, perhaps her other daughter might actually be happy in a loving home.

On the bus trip home, Rita finally came to terms with what she had done. It wasn't peace she felt, but a grim resolution. She would stop pining away for her husband and find a father for Mina. How to find a suitable husband was unclear, but she had to find someone since her mother was getting older and wouldn't be able to help with Mina much longer.

Rita vowed to find an eligible man. Once married, she could take care of Mina herself rather than relying on her mother. There had to be someone somewhere, perhaps outside of Schlangenbad, where her past didn't cling to her like a second skin.

She decided to travel to the village of Buchloe on weekends and established a regular pattern of coming to and from home. Gertrude, a friend from primary school who had moved to Buchloe three years before, might be able to help. As predicted, Gertrude stepped up.

Rita spent the night on her visits, and Gertrude introduced her to new friends.

In town, Rita walked the streets visiting shops. On every recurring visit, she made a point of going to the same spot for lunch. Soon, the locals got to know her. She asked if she could make ice cream in their shops. They, like Gertrude, were accommodating.

Before summer's end, Rita became reacquainted with Gertrude's brother, Fritz. They had not seen each other in years. He was a bit older and had married a lovely woman from Buchloe. Fritz mentioned that their friend Dieter might get along well with Rita, but he was a widower and carried a shadow of grief wherever he went.

There weren't very many single people left in Rita's age group. He was ten years her senior. Perhaps they could help each other mend their broken souls. Fritz arranged a casual group dinner at the local pub.

The months sped by. Rita and Dieter enjoyed each other's company within the group, but they had not gone on any solo dates. They had shared many conversations covering their day-to-day experiences. Dieter took a particularly long time to open up about his wife's death. When he did, he explained she'd died from complications related to appendicitis. He felt responsible for not taking the warning signs seriously. The loss haunted him.

Rita didn't tell Dieter about the baby she had outside of marriage and gave away. That truly was too heavy to hand over. She was getting impatient with the evolution of their relationship. She had grown to love him, but she was not in love. Perhaps given enough time alone, her feelings would change. She knew Dieter needed to meet Mina, who was a three-year-old and a handful. So far, he had accepted the idea, but a meeting in person would be the final test. After a great deal of thought, Rita decided to bring Mina on her next visit to Buchloe.

Mina was so excited to take the bus to Buchloe, but for Rita, the ride stirred old ghosts of their trip together to the convent the year before. Mina stood on the seat the same way she had done before, with her eyes glowing with happiness, while she watched the scenery go by. She was oblivious to her mother's sorrows.

When they passed pastures of cows and other animals, Mina kept saying over and over, "Mamma, look…" She had never been exposed to so many. That was the day Mina fell in love with animals.

They walked into Buchloe to Gertrude's home. Mina was greeted with open arms, but she was a bit shy and clung to her mother's leg. An hour later, Gertrude was reading her a children's story. While they rested, Rita slipped out to make some ice cream at the nearby shop and pick up a few things for the evening party. She returned to find Mina curled up on the couch, sound asleep.

Rita and Gertrude got to work in the kitchen. The six guests arrived shortly thereafter. Dieter would finally meet little Mina, but Rita was nervous. Her daughter was not like most children because she learned more from her grandmother than her mother and often behaved like a little adult. Rita needed this evening to go well. She needed Dieter to see Mina for the angel she was before the school year began. They would have to move to Buchloe and start a new life.

Mina began the evening sitting on Rita's lap, but soon warmed up to all the guests. She showed each of them her new stuffed bear from Gertrude. Everything seemed to be going well.

"Mina, go get a book and bring it back." Off she trotted and returned with a book of photographs.

Rita was wondering what Dieter would do. She wasn't sure, but soon discovered he was quite interested in the book and offered to go through it with Mina. He leaned in closer than she expected. He asked questions. He listened. This, Rita thought, could be the next step, and it was. Dieter asked Rita out on a real date before he left. He had not done so before because he said the mysterious child had created an obstacle in his mind.

Rita and Dieter went on their first date, and then another and another. Their relationship developed, and Dieter soon learned to love again. The love between Dieter and Rita was not full of sparks, but a love of understanding. The losses they had incurred made them older and wiser than they actually were. She was now twenty-five, and he was thirty-five.

They agreed to start a life together. Dieter bought a small house with plenty of room for the three of them with room to grow. The property had a spacious yard and a separate building. He was handy with tools and planned to convert the building into an ice cream shop for Rita. A gesture both loving and conveniently located. But he resisted the idea of Mina coming to live with them right away. He wanted them to spend the summer alone.

The renovations were taking longer than expected, and it was time for Mina to start school. They decided she should stay in Schlangenbad with Grandmother Magda. Mina could join them on school breaks and move permanently to Buchloe later on. At this point, Rita knew the drawn-out renovations were an excuse on Dieter's part, but she reluctantly accepted the situation. Maybe too easily. After all, Magda had spent more time with Mina than she had. Rita promised to visit them often.

But as the months passed, a quiet ache grew. Rita knew Dieter didn't really understand what it meant to be a parent. He didn't see Mina very often, but when he did, he was aloof since he didn't know how to relate to her as a stepfather. It didn't help that Rita continued to travel back and forth from Buchloe to Schlangenbad on a regular basis to see Mina.

He often said he was jealous of the child and hoped to feel more complete with a child of his own. He didn't have to fret for very long. Rita became pregnant with his child. Dieter was elated with the news, but his negative behavior toward Mina remained constant.

Mina became confused by her mother's growing belly. She wanted a brother or sister, but she didn't understand why she lived with her grandmother. By this time, Mina was almost six years old.

"Mina, I have to tell you something important. After you were born, I had another baby. I couldn't keep her with me or your grandmother because we did not have enough money."

Mina's wide eyes filled with tears. "Mama, are you going to give me away too? Are you going to keep this baby?"

In some ways, Rita had given Mina away to her mother. "No, little one, I am not going to give either of you away. We have money now."

"Mama, where do babies come from?"

"You will understand when you are older. We will not talk about this today. Think about what I've already said."

Mina's world was splintered. She often asked about her lost sister. "Where is my sister? I want my sister! You are so mean! I will be angry with you forever!"

Rita didn't try to silence her daughter. She let Mina's anger roll over her like a deserved wave.

Another Baby

Rita gave birth to a third daughter; they named her Eva. Dieter was a proud father, but he was away many hours each day minding the local hardware store and taking odd handyman jobs in the neighborhood. It was difficult for them to pay the bills. Sending money to Schlangenbad each month for Mina became a source of resentment. He gazed at his daughter one morning. "You're my light, Eva. The only thing that reminds me of what hope feels like." His voice softened as he tucked a strand of her baby-fine hair behind her ear, the weight of his life disappointments pressing down on him.

Four years flew quickly by. The ice cream business was so busy in the summers that Rita needed extra help that her now four-year-old, Eva, couldn't provide. Gertrude helped serve on Sundays, which was a great relief.

Rita had finished three new batches of ice cream when she heard the phone ringing in the house. She ran inside and picked up the receiver.

"Hello?"

"Frau Richter?"

"Yes?"

"I am calling from Mina's school, you need to come get her. Your mother fell in the market. She's been admitted to the hospital. We haven't told Mina anything."

"Yes, I understand. I will be there as soon as I can."

"No, you need to be here when school lets out for the day." The administrator insisted.

Rita barely knew how to handle this new development. She rushed back to Gertrude. "My mother is in the hospital. I need to go. Can you manage things here? I have to do something with Mina. I will telephone you later."

Gertrude responded as any friend would. "Go. We will get through this."

Rita left Eva with Gertrude and hurried off to the hardware store to talk to Dieter.

He flinched and said, "We knew this day would come." He turned and walked toward the back room. His reaction was cold. "Handle it, Rita. I can't leave work now." She turned away, fearing the worst.

Rita jumped on the bus to Schlangenbad and arrived with only a few minutes to spare before Mina walked out of school. They would go to the hospital together.

"Mama, what are you doing here?"

The interaction was strained; Rita didn't know how to explain why she was there unannounced. "It's my turn to pick you up after school." Her voice trembled.

They walked for a few minutes without speaking of anything

except for the events that occurred during Mina's school day, while Rita tried to figure out how to explain.

Rita hailed a taxi cab and abruptly told the driver to go to the hospital. This was the first clue for Mina.

"Mama, what's wrong?"

"Your grandmother was at the market and fell. The shopkeeper said she needed to go to the hospital. So, she went. Someone from school called me. That is why I am here to pick you up today instead."

"No! Grandmama can't be hurt…She's always fine."

"Let's go see how she's feeling."

When they arrived at the hospital, Mina had to wait in the lobby, because they wouldn't permit her in Magda's room. She sat on a bench while Rita went to speak with the doctor.

"Your mother had a stroke and can't speak…. She will not recover completely…. If she is stable in a week or so, we will need to move her to a nursing home."

Rita felt the room tilt slightly beneath her. She was suddenly zapped of all her energy. In her mother's room, Rita pulled up a chair and scowled while she figured out what to do next. Her mother was unresponsive. Fifteen minutes later, she went back out to Mina.

"Mama, I've been waiting and waiting for you to come back. Is Grandmama going to be all right?"

"She fell because her brain stopped working properly. She can't speak anymore; she had a stroke."

Mina broke down. "A-a-a stroke? What is that? What will happen to her?"

"It's difficult to explain. The hospital will move her to another home for nursing care for the rest of her life, and you will move in with me and Dieter in Buchloe."

"Noooo, I don't want to leave grandmama." She began to sob convulsively. "I want to stay with her and go to school with my friends."

"I know things seem horrible right now. I will stay with you both for the rest of the school year. In the summer, you will have to leave with me."

Mina pulled away from her mother and ran down the hall to her grandmother's room. Rita rushed after her as a nurse attempted to stop Mina in mid stride.

"Child, child, you cannot go in there. Hospital rules say…." The nurse's voice caught and faltered.

Rita and the nurse plunged into the room simultaneously. They froze in their tracks when they saw how quiet and statue-like Mina had become. She reached out and touched Magda's hand. Magda opened her eyes, and her mouth twitched. An indiscernible sound emerged.

"Mina, she needs to rest. Let's go and get things organized at her house."

"I'll help you, Mama. I'll always help, even if no one sees."

"You're precious," Rita said. "I am sorry. I know this is very difficult for you."

"Grandmama, I love you. See you later." Mina reluctantly left, while her world crumbled. She was only eight years old, and she had been through too much.

Grandmother Magda was dead within the month. Rita telephoned home, and Dieter sounded rather agitated. He and Gertrude had been taking care of both Eva and the ice cream shop while she was away. They were exhausted and wanted her to return, but school wouldn't be over for another six weeks.

Dieter soon found himself a full-time father of another man's child. He thought it wouldn't bother him, but deep down, he was uneasy, conflicted in a way he couldn't shake. He loved his bride, but he really didn't want to be the father of someone else's daughter. He continued to try to relate to Mina, but reading to her at bedtime was the only connection he could manage. A ritual without warmth.

"Stop looking at me like that, Mina. Like you're waiting for something that isn't coming." He turned away, his voice sharper than he intended, the anger masking a guilt that gnawed at him. He wasn't committed to her like he was to his Eva. He decided he would spend more hours working while Mina settled into their home with Eva. He told himself time would help. Distance even more. God willing, he could think things through and get used to the idea of the alien child. He didn't like the thoughts that plagued his mind—resentment, pity, rejection. He knew what he was getting into the day he married Rita. But knowing and living it turned out to be two different things. Dieter doted on Eva, lavishing her with attention— reading to her, telling her stories, and giving her little wooden toys he'd carved for her in the evenings. All these things Mina noticed with glaring stares, but she never said a word.

Mina wanted to love her baby sister, but she was jealous. Over and over, she stood back and watched the family of three and wondered where she fit. Was she a freak? A leftover? A reminder of something no one wanted to remember? Her life could be complete if her lost sister returned. They were so close in age—eighteen months—and in circumstances. Mina knew they would have had each other to depend on. A shield against Dieter's indifference.

Rita attended to Eva, while Mina helped with the ice cream business, went to school, and did household chores. By the time she was ten and Eva was four, Dieter began to drink too much and put fewer hours in at work. They needed more money to support four people, so Rita tried to relieve him of his burden by keeping Mina out of his path, as if hiding her might calm his riddled soul. But the storm never ceased. He was a selfish man.

They worked harder selling ice cream, but money was still scarce. There wasn't an immediate solution, not until Rita heard the government was looking for foster families to care for abandoned children. There were so many in Germany who needed homes and not enough families who could adopt them within the country. Many of the children were living in overcrowded orphanages with poor conditions. Rita believed she could give back something to these children, perhaps even make peace with the parts of herself that had given one of her own away. The one Dieter still didn't know about. He agreed to foster some, but only because they needed more money and the government would pay them for their cooperation.

By the end of the month, there were three more children in their home, and Rita was determined to make a happier life for them all.

But the duties of the house multiplied, and Mina quickly became the house's Cinderella. She swept, she served, and tended to her studies. When time allowed (there was very little), she tried to spend it with friends. Rita watched her daughter trying to keep an upbeat attitude, trying not to anger Dieter, but he was never satisfied—not with her, not with anything.

The money was flowing into the house, but Dieter still behaved like a stranger in his own home. He spent most of his time either working, playing with Eva or drinking more and more alcohol. He became so dependent on his nightly beers that he was drinking away a lot of the extra income Rita had been bringing in with the foster children. To protect the household, she had to find ways to hide a portion of the money so the children would have enough food and clothing. There were days Dieter became verbally aggressive and was known to throw a thing or two across the room. A glass, a book. Once, a shoe. Anything within reach. He became more and more difficult to live with.

"Do you think I want this life, Rita? Do you think I don't see what I've become?" Dieter's voice cracked as he clenched an empty glass, his face flushed with something between rage and despair.

Rita regretted the day she thought a new husband would make their life better—he hadn't made it better. He was not the right man for her or for Mina. She was stuck in her Catholic principles and would never leave him. Divorce was not an option. She didn't pray for deliverance anymore, only for strength. Her sentence would be over soon enough; the liquor was sure to kill him.

Mina felt helpless, but she continued to help her mother and became a surrogate to the three foster children. Her life was filled with school, work, and almost no time with friends. Often, she cried herself to sleep at night, clutching her pillow while dreaming of a sister she had never met. Mina wished she had been sent away for adoption, too. At least then, she imagined, someone might have chosen her. Life was too hard, and Eva seemed to get everything she wanted—new toys, attention, affection. Mina was left with nothing but work.

NUNS AND SOLDIERS – MINA'S COMPOSITION

Mina, now in upper school, walked into the building. She was late—by two weeks and many hours. It was the end of the day, and her last class would start in ten minutes. Creative writing was her favorite subject. She quietly entered the room, slipping past the teacher, Frau Becker, who paused a moment to speak while maneuvering around the desk at the front of the room.

Frau Becker glanced at her clipboard, furrowing her brow. "Mina? Hmm, you're not on my list." She stuck her head out into the hall, calling out, "Frau Hermann, do you have Mina in your class?"

"Oh, yes," came a response from across the hall.

Mina cringed. She recognized Frau Hermann's voice. Of the two teachers, Frau Becker was her favorite. Gossip about Frau Hermann wasn't kind.

"Go to Frau Hermann. I'm sure you can write volumes after your summer break."

Mina sighed and made her way across the hall, taking the only remaining seat at the front of the room. Her classmates snickered.

"All right class," Frau Hermann said, her voice sharp and stern. "In our last session, we began a composition about the outdoors. I want you to continue writing."

Her gaze fixed directly on Mina. "There are no additional guidelines for this assignment. Use your imagination—write what you want. Ask questions if you need to, but we won't be reading excerpts out loud until the next class. The writing must be at least two hand-written pages. You may speak to your neighbors about your story, but nothing else."

"Yes, Frau Hermann." The class chimed in unison, their voices flat.

Frau Hermann opened a book, her head twitching as she turned the pages.

It didn't take long for Mina to decide how to approach the 'outdoor' assignment, except she wasn't going to write about her summer travels, as Frau Hermann suggested. She hadn't traveled at all. The entire summer—and the last two weeks—had been spent tending to her mother's foster kids. It hadn't been fun; not really. She began frantically writing a rough draft, deciding to worry about the details later. Mina wasn't sure why, but instead of writing from her native land's point of view, she'd tell it from a French perspective. Here is what she wrote…

Four young men, dressed in ragged, ill-fitting disguises, struggled to focus on something besides their emerging hunger. Their faded green jackets and makeshift rucksacks bore the signs of long journeys through the occupied countryside. They trudged along a narrow, winding dirt road that cut through the rolling fields of northern France while distant sounds of artillery and sporadic gunfire echoed across the land.

The previous day's rain had left the road muddy with deeply carved ruts, created primarily by German convoys. Their boots, caked in mud, squelched as they trudged on. On either side of the road, fields of tall wheat and rye swayed in the breeze, providing possible cover for the men from any prying eyes. They broke off a few tops of the wheat and chewed the tough, sweet pieces to stave off their hunger, and cursed each other for not bringing along enough provisions while they continued along the road. Then, not long after, the unmistakable sound of marching German boots grew louder behind them. Quickly, they ducked into the tall grasses, holding their breath as the footsteps came closer and closer. Getting shot wasn't part of the plan.

"Hey, you there!" a commanding voice shouted from the front of the line of a dozen soldiers, first in German and then in French. "Come out. What are you doing there?"

The young men threw their rucksacks aside, smeared dirt on their faces, and slowly emerged from the grass with their heads held down. Badeaux, the boldest of the group, stepped forward, and added a tremor to his voice. "Nothing sirs. Just playing."

The leader stood still, his hard gaze appearing to assess the young men before him. Instead of shooting them, he said, "Go home. These roads are no place for children's games. Times like these…." His voice trailed off.

Grabbing their rucksacks, the relieved young men scurried away into the grasses. They had survived the encounter. They were thankful their disguise had worked. Children they were not. Yet, their ages were hidden behind faces that were perpetually youthful. A fortunate quirk of ancestry had granted them this particular blessing, and they'd exploited it at every opportunity.

When the road was clear, they resumed their journey. They were on a mission, not for play, but to protect. Their orders had come from their captain—to protect the nuns and children in a distant church hidden deep in the woodlands. The road was treacherous, but there was no turning back.

Further down the road, they reached the edge of the woods. Garnier, the tallest and most agile of the three, climbed a tree to get a better view of the land. Beyond the trees, his keen eyes spotted a stone bridge arching over a narrow river, leading to another dense patch of trees.

Sliding down the tree, Garnier made his report to the others. "If we move slowly, and stay low, the meadow's grasses should help camouflage us."

The others nodded. Fournier, always quick with a joke, gave a half-hearted salute before they pressed on. The ground was softer than the road they had left behind, but their boots didn't sink through the debris made from years of rotting grasses. After about an hour of slow progress, they reached the stone bridge and hid beneath it just as an enemy battalion rumbled overhead. They waited in silence and remained unnoticed. As soon as the way was clear, they took a moment to pull out a map and check their compass bearings. They had a few miles to go. Before moving on, they filled their canteens with the crystal-clear water from the stream, dropping iodine tablets in to kill any bacteria. Their thirst was so great that they didn't take the time to let the bitterness of the iodine fade. They consumed the remaining portions of their dry biscuits and dehydrated meat, washing them down with the pungent water before setting off again.

Within two hours, they reached the church. Its ancient stone building had divots in the worn walls. The bells were tied to the tower to prevent them from ringing and bringing attention to its inhabitants. Above the heavy oak doors, adorned with twisted iron bands in Gothic shapes, sat a statue of a saint. Vines crawled up the sides, gripping the stones. Nuns, their faces lined with exhaustion, greeted them, followed by a group of children whose eyes were wide with either fear or curiosity. Protecting children was a surprise and had not been part of their orders, but the Mother Superior explained that the church was the only safe place for miles. There was nowhere else for the children to go. The young men handed over their written orders to a nun and followed them into the church, verifying their identity and explaining their purpose. Their purpose was to protect the building's inhabitants.

The building felt colder than the outside air. The vaulted ceilings arched high above, supported by massive columns. Streaks of pale light filtered through the stained-glass windows; their once-vibrant colors dulled by layers of grime. Candles melted down to meager stubs lined the aisles. Up behind the altar loomed a crucifix, adorned with a figure of Christ carved with painstaking detail.

As the young soldiers adjusted to their new surroundings, they noticed a small classroom in an alcove. Rough wooden benches sat around wooden tables. Children's charcoal drawings, made from scraps of paper, lined the walls—images of homes, animals, and family members untouched by war. Dolls, dressed in miniature uniforms and finery, lay scattered across the tables, alongside scraps of fabric and dress-up clothing. On a blackboard, a note said, Let's create a world where you can imagine yourselves as adults.

It was a world of imagination and escape, but beneath it, the weight of the war loomed. The soldiers could almost hear the echoes of the children's voices as they played out their dreams. Conflicts between them would arise. The line between imagination and reality would blur.

Over the next two days, the soldiers had plenty of time to rest and get to know their surroundings. They wanted to gain their host's trust while they took turns sleeping and keeping watch over the grounds, which included a dormitory and a barn. The dormitory was filled end to end with two lines of metal framed beds, spaced two feet apart, with a nightstand in between each bed. Each bed had a wooden trunk at its foot that resembled a military style footlocker. Some beds had handmade colorful quilts, while others had a stuffed animal resting on the pillow. Each special addition had been brought by a child when he or she had to take shelter with the nuns.

The barn stood behind the church, a humble structure that had weathered decades with surprising resilience. Its sloped thatched roof sagged slightly in the middle, as if burdened by the weight of the seasons. Moss and ivy crept up the stone and wood walls. Double doors hung unevenly on their iron hinges; one door slightly ajar. Inside the dimly lit barn, the wooden crossbeams were darkened and splintered in places. Empty sacks dangled from hooks and twitched in a barely perceptible draft. Wooden slatted box stalls lined the walls in two rows on either side of an uneven packed dirt floor that was smooth in places from years of hooves and footsteps. The scene reminded the men of the children's beds for reasons they could not pinpoint. Some stalls had horses, others housed cows or goats when they weren't out in the pastures. Above the stalls was a loft as long as the building, with an access ladder hidden within a closet at the far end of the building. The loft was stacked with bales of hay and loose piles of straw. The smell of old straw, wood, and earth filled the air, mixed with the scent of animals.

The men's sense of security soon vanished when Badeaux spotted a group of seedy looking, scraggly troops appearing on the horizon.

"They're not friendly," he muttered, and woke the other men.

Quickly, they gathered the children from the dormitory, guided them into the barn's loft, and covered them with straw. Small gaps in the walls provided a glimpse of the outside world—the tops of trees swaying in the wind, the rolling fields beyond, and distant smoke from unknown sources. A beam of light came through a corner of the ceiling, revealing dust particles that had been stirred up when the men covered the children.

"Stay completely still and quiet, Badeaux whispered before rushing to join the others, weapons in hand. The young men took their positions on either side of the arches of the stone entrance and waited...

The bell rang. Mina extracted herself from the words on the page. She closed her notebook before standing and leaving the room. Another day she might finish her story. Or maybe this was really the end. She thought *readers will have to take this tale on further with their own imaginations.* But for her, it was a retelling of a relative's experience during the war. A story she had been told, but as far as the class was concerned, it was a fictional tale.

A NIGHT AT BLOB'S PARK

Having nothing better to do, Heidi tagged along with her parents to a cocktail party. It was the usual scene: clinking glasses, polite laughter, and clusters of people murmuring about business, politics, and the mundane dramas of upper crust society. She'd acquired a glass of red wine from the bar and swirled the contents around, while trying to blend into the ornate wallpaper and disappear. The evening stretched on uneventfully until a man with a thick German accent appeared by her side, singing under his breath.

Heidi had never seen him before within any of her parents' circles of friends or at any embassy function that she'd been obliged to attend. His name was Claus. Not a particularly tall man. Maybe he was five-foot-eight or so. His hair, unlike Heidi's, was blonde and cropped short against his pale scalp. Despite his otherwise unassuming appearance, something about him unsettled her.

"Pleasure to meet you, Heidi," Claus said, his voice warm but edged with something she couldn't quite place. How did he know her name? Throughout the evening, they spoke at length, his stories veering from tales of his youth in Germany to accounts of his love of dancing. As the party was coming to an end, Claus announced he was going to Blob's Park for a German meal and dance event in the coming days. He went every month, and his dance partner wasn't available this time around. With a charming smile, he invited Heidi. At first, she was a little hesitant due to his age. But before she could refuse, her mother swooped in with her socialite enthusiasm.

"Oh, Heidi, you must go!" her mother gushed. "It will be so much fun. An adventure to be had.

Heidi sighed inwardly, cursing her mother's obsession with propriety, and reluctantly agreed.

A week later, Claus came by her parent's home in a polished black sedan. A sinking feeling gripped her stomach as she slid into the passenger seat. The drive to Blob's Park took forty-five minutes and led down country roads she'd never seen before. Tall trees cast shadows that crisscrossed the road as the sun set. She clutched her purse a little tighter. Claus's conversation, though friendly, did little to calm her nerves. He seemed nice enough, but something about him felt slightly off. All the scary movies she's watched down country lanes started to get under her skin.

She'd never traveled away from home with anyone but her parents and attempted to distract her mind from the unfamiliar situation. Blob's Park, what a strange name. Was it named after a Mr. Blob? If it was, he was probably teased as a kid.

Finally, he pulled the car into the gravel parking lot of Blob's Park in what appeared to be in the remote outskirts of Jessup, Maryland. The place had a kind of old-world charm with a Tudor-style façade adorned with flower boxes bursting with bright red geraniums. Strings of white fairy lights hung over the entrance. An old wooden sign read *Blob's Park* in bold letters with the subtitle *Bavarian Dance Hall*.

"This is an institution with decades of memories of polka, waltzes, and laughter for every attendant," Claus said with a hop in his step.

"Blob's Park," Heidi murmured, taking in the building's appearance. The oddness of the situation caused her to shiver when Claus placed his hand on her back as they entered.

Inside, the atmosphere buzzed with life. A hostess greeted

them at the door of the hall. Wrought-iron chandeliers hung from the vaulted ceiling. An enormous dance floor filled the center of the room, surrounded by people chatting and clinking steins of beer together. A mural of the Bavarian Alps stretched across one wall, making the place feel as if it had been plucked straight from Europe and dropped into rural Maryland.

The hostess took them to a long wooden table draped with red-and-white checkered tablecloths by the edge of the dance floor. Pre-arranged German beers and plates of sauerkraut with bratwurst were placed in front of them. Heidi had barely taken a bite before a voice from an overhead speaker asked the guests to enjoy their meals while music played in the background. They said the show would begin shortly. After they finished eating, musicians emerged from back rooms pulling instruments on wheels resembling enormous corncob pipes that extended ten-feet across the floor. Claus informed her they were called Alpenhorns. The thunderous notes reverberated through the hall, rattling the glasses and echoing in her chest. The performance was followed by cloggers, whose lively rhythmic tapping filled the room. Next, high school age kids came onto the dance floor, demonstrating German folk dances in traditional Bavarian costumes. The dancers departed. Finally, the music softened and continued at a reduced volume in the background. Coffee and dessert were brought out by servers dressed in costume. The air smelled of cinnamon and freshly brewed coffee, but Heidi found it hard to relax. She preferred small gatherings with activities and people she knew. This situation was beyond her experience. She tapped her foot out of sight under the table, attempting to follow the beat of the music instead of showing her true angst by voicing her objections to the entire scene.

Someone turned up the music, and an announcer invited everyone to dance. Claus stood and offered his hand to Heidi. He guided her onto the floor with confidence and grace, leading her through waltz after waltz, his movement smooth and practiced. She felt like a clumsy child, but Claus's calm direction kept her from stumbling too badly. Initially, she wasn't sure how to respond, as she'd never been taught any type of formal dancing, much less danced with an older man who was not her father. The memory of dancing with him drifted into view. She'd stood on her dad's feet as a child while moving through the steps with him. The recollection brought a smile across her face that Claus seemed to appreciate, even though it had nothing to do with him.

At the end of the evening, she was more than ready to go home and still felt odd about going to a dance with a man who must have been at least fifty. She couldn't shake the feeling that this whole outing had been a mistake. Claus guided her back to the car, but instead of retracing the now familiar route, he turned down a narrow road.

"Where are we going?" she asked, trying to keep her voice steady.

Claus didn't respond right away. He stopped in front of an old stone building with a dilapidated sign dangling from one of the two hooks. Looking sideways at the crooked letters, she reads *Saint Francis' Orphanage*. At that moment, her skin prickled and she thought of horror stories once again. Then Claus told her why they were there.

"It was closed a decade ago," he said quietly. "When I visited the nuns years back, I was quite disappointed that the place was empty. It was the last place I saw my baby girl."

Heidi stiffened, and her throat tightened. What was happening? Heidi knew she had been adopted, but this announcement didn't make a bit of sense to her.

"I had to leave her," Claus continued, his voice cracking. "I couldn't raise her alone."

"Take me home," she demanded. "I've heard enough."

Circling the conversation back to the dance, Claus said,

"Soon, soon. I enjoyed the special evening we shared and wished we could spend more time together."

Now she was really creeped out. She wanted nothing more than to be taken home and never see this peculiar man again. What had her mother been thinking when she encouraged her to go to Blob's Park? After all, the park wasn't too far away from the prison. Could he be a recently released convict? No, her mother would never have suggested she go along.

"I wanted to say…" Claus began.

Taking a deep breath, Heidi waited to hear what Claus would come up with, but he was staring out the window with his mouth open, as if he's been stupefied. Finally, he told her what their evening was all about.

"I'm sorry," he said. "I never should have left you."

"What?"

"Your mother was gone and—and I left you, too. I left you here."

"You're crazy," she said. "Take me home."

"No, it's true. You were only six months old. I couldn't take care of you. Your parents, your dedicated parents, adopted you from this orphanage a few months later. I was able to find you through archived records. After that, I contacted your parents, and they agreed to help me. That is why I showed up at that cocktail party where I first met you."

"No!" Heidi's voice shook. "Why didn't they warn me instead of sending me off dancing?"

"Truthfully, they wanted us to spend some time together before I told you."

"Not their best plan. I'll need some time to absorb all this. Please, just take me home so I can talk this over with them."

"Understandable. I'm sorry for everything."

The weight of his confession hung heavily between them. The night felt colder, heavier, and more complicated than it had been only a few hours before. Finally, he started the car, his hands trembling on the wheel. He drove her home in silence, neither one knowing if they would ever meet again.

∽

Footnote: Blob's Park in Jessup, Maryland, closed permanently in 2014 after eighty-one years in business.

THE WHITE DRESS
SENSITIVE PIECE

On the bedroom wall hung a long, white gown with buttons and a concealed zipper running down the back. Heidi gingerly slid it off the hanger, gathered it up and pulled it over her head, before smoothing the fabric in long stroking movements. She walked over to the full-length mirror in her room, which shared a door into the bathroom, and gazed at her reflection. Her breath caught; this was the moment she'd dreamed of, yet it felt foreign. Her focus was so intense that she was startled when her father walked in with a rose and an envelope from her future husband. The enclosed note brought a smile to her face, and she tucked it into her bra. After refocusing on her father, she asked him to fasten the back of the gown. Once done, she adjusted the hem and pulled on a previously styled, full-length wig to disguise her short hair for the walk down the aisle. When she peered back in the mirror, a memory surged into her consciousness, unwelcome and sharp.

In the flashback, a young man loomed over her. She remembered seeing a naked man years before during her innocent youth through a cracked door—but not like this, not partially dressed and erect. He moved towards her, speaking in a soothing, coaxing voice. He pulled her to the ground. Tears flowed with the ignorance of the act he was attempting to perform. They were both drunk, but that didn't lessen the consequences.

Trying to escape the image, she turned around and looked straight into her father's eyes, but was shaken to see the same face from her memory, blurred by time. The young man from her 18-year-old self had merged with the trusted one standing before her. Shame and confusion rippled through her, making her question everything again.

The truth had come crashing down on her on the one day she should be celebrating. In that moment, the loneliness was suffocating. She didn't understand the feeling. So alone while her father stood next to her. So alone while her mother was fussing over fashion and her own losses in another room. So alone while her best girlfriend was not by her side. Claudia's absence was deserved. Heidi had been late to the church rehearsal when Claudia married two years before. Now, this absence felt like karma, or was it a punishment? Perhaps it wasn't, but Heidi felt abandoned without her.

Heidi knew more about sex than she thought she should in her twenty-seventh year. It had all started out wrong. The journey had been fraught with fears and confusion, starting with the day she'd learned of her adoption when she was a baby. She was thirteen when the truth was revealed. That day and all days going forward, she'd wondered if she had siblings in Germany and what their lives were like. Had their lives been worse or the same? Had they made better decisions, had better outcomes?

She kept coming back to the night everything had gone wrong. That night, one beer at a time, she'd gotten drunk and met a stranger. That night, in a broom closet, they had fumbled in a haze of alcohol and poor decisions. The only saving grace was that he was a friend's friend, so she rationalized he wasn't quite a stranger. But this wasn't how her first encounter was supposed to be. It was supposed to be with a deep, mutual love that her church and her mother would approve.

Discussions with her mother about growing up had never been easy. The first about menstruation after it had started. The second at sixteen, when she had received a book from a classmate that contained what she now knew as soft porn. The book was stimulating. She wrote a note to her classmate with questions about birth control and threw it in the trash can in her room instead of delivering it. Her mother, snooping through the trash, found the note. That night, her mother confronted her ranting about abstinence and consequences. Shame and fear were weapons wielded to ensure obedience. All the while, Heidi wondered if her first mother would have talked to her this way. Wondered if her existence began with an unforeseen sexual liaison that ended in pregnancy. Perhaps the ranting was well placed to keep Heidi from making the same mistakes. Perhaps her adopted mother and father knew the truth. By the end of the pointed, repetitive remarks, she forbade Heidi from speaking to her classmate again.

Heidi grew up attending a conservative church, where she became a 'born-again' Christian after reconfirming her faith in Jesus, in God, as well as learning many of the lessons in the Bible. The youth group became her lifeline in a social circle that rooted her in a community that felt uncomplicated and secure. Unlike her school surroundings on weekdays, where peer rivalries and struggles with classwork were daunting.

When she started driving, her mother set down strict rules saying she could only go on double dates. Even then, she had a curfew. The rest of the time, she was expected to focus on her studies and distance herself from her girlfriends. The very friends who had been her refuge throughout her academic life. No outings. No sleepovers. Her friends couldn't understand why Heidi—so quiet, obedient, and naïve—didn't rebel against the new rules. To them, it felt like a betrayal. Most of them drifted away, hurt and confused. Only Claudia remained.

At first, Heidi felt so alone until the guys at school began visiting her at her locker. Flattered by the attention, she mistook their intentions for genuine interest. Guys she'd never associated with before. Some became real friends, and others wanted to tease and play. Caught in a cycle of seeking validation, she was bringing to life the words in a song by Johnny Lee, *Looking for Love in All the Wrong Places*. That night at the party was the night she spiraled onto an unintended path. She'd interpreted her church teachings to mean she was stuck with the guy for life because they'd had sex at the party. In her mind, they were effectively married—without legal documents. On their first official date, he came towards her again at the end of the evening, and they both disrobed. In the midst of his seduction, she felt a pain and a pop while realizing he hadn't taken her virginity when they were drunk. Before that very moment, she had no obligation to him. Now she did, and he didn't feel the same way. He said he just wanted to have fun and go their separate ways when school was over.

A few months before prom, Heidi pulled herself together. She avoided going on any more dates. He didn't agree with the separation. Then, just two weeks before prom, he forced himself on her at his best friend's house. She didn't understand why he had chosen that place, or if he had thought about it at all. Perhaps it was a twisted attempt to punish his friend for asking her to the prom. None of it made sense. She realized she would never know what drove him to lose control.

After the assault, Heidi didn't know who to turn to for help. The church wasn't an option. Her parents and friends weren't an option. Her response, however illogical, was to get a new boyfriend who didn't know what had happened as quickly as possible. Then another and another all through college while trying to find resolution and love, again *in all the wrong* places, instead of immersing herself in studies that would lead to a profitable career. The concept was somewhat new to her since her mother was a homemaker, as were most women of her mother's generation. Heidi was lost and deeply hurt on all fronts. One day, she thought, one day, she would find a proper love, a proper man, to restore her faith in humanity. Until then, she would be somewhere between Hell and damnation.

Today, standing in her wedding gown, she felt that day had finally come. But the flashback in the mirror was in danger of ruining a perfect day in the white dress her mother said she didn't deserve to wear.

THE MESSY ART OF LIVING

What were the odds that Heidi would have three—no, numerous—mishaps in one day? That was a foolish question, she was sure. When she gave up her office job, she never imagined family events could be so chaotic.

Their eldest daughter, now in her early teens, had moved to a room in the basement that Heidi had recently painted with a sand-textured tan paint, highlighted by dark green rafters. She approached her daughter's room and called out, "Good morning, time for school." While surveying the cluttered hallway, she realized she needed to pick up everything before the bimonthly house cleaner arrived. She only had an hour to prepare. Heidi grabbed a half empty paint can by the stairwell. The handle broke loose, and the can fell on her foot. Her daughter didn't come out of her room to help when Heidi began cursing at the pain. Luckily, the younger children, who were upstairs eating breakfast, didn't hear her string of expletives.

After taking a few deep breaths, Heidi called out, "Are you ready for school?"

"Mom, I'm getting dressed."

The sound of Madonna's song, "Don't Tell Me" drifted out of the room along with her eldest daughter's laughter.

"What's with all the giggles? Hurry up."

She came out into the hall singing along with Madonna holding a banana posing as a microphone, and dressed all in black. A new look. Colorful clothing became a thing of the past.

"Really?" Heidi couldn't quite take it all in at first. She tried not to sneer or get angry. The Goth look went well with their daughter's fair skin, but the culture connected to it worried Heidi. Next thing she knew, her daughter would be screaming Heavy Metal songs instead of Madonna's or adding piercings to her new style. It was just a matter of time.

"Yeah, no biggie. Mom, I'm just trying something new."

"Go on upstairs and see if your sibs are done with breakfast. It's almost time to catch the bus." Heidi looked at her daughter's face. "And rub the black lipstick off or I will."

"Yes, ma'am."

Knowing she still had a million things to clean up, Heidi hurried to the freezer in the hall closet and grabbed some frozen cubed beef to carry up to the kitchen. If she didn't plan dinner in the morning, life would turn into a new form of chaos. She had to dig deep into the freezer to get the package out. Her hands tingled. The package was almost too cold to handle. The lid swung down and hit her head. More curse words disappeared into the frozen mist.

Upstairs, the children were absorbed in their own world, bustling around the table, shoving things in their backpacks, and talking about the day ahead. By the time they got out the door and onto the bus, Heidi was ready for some personal therapy—or at the very least, a distraction from her bruised foot—so she headed to the public barn for her weakly horseback righting lessons.

Riding in the woods on the trails would have been preferable, but the group lesson on this particular day was in the arena. The day's routine began with grooming, tacking, and mounting the horse. They went around and around with their instructor shouting out various instructions. Then she stopped the group and told them to try some new stretching exercises while sitting in the saddle. Next thing Heidi knew, she'd put both feet on the saddle with her knees on either side of her chin. She couldn't quite get her knees to her ears as instructed. The horse appeared unfazed and didn't move during the maneuvers.

Katja, her photographer friend, said, "I would have loved to have my camera right now." They all laughed. Heidi enjoyed entertaining people, but they often didn't catch her intended humor. This time they got it.

The week before, Donna and Heidi had gone to their bimonthly midday movie outing, followed by a meal and discussion. The movie gave Heidi an idea. She had to share it with her riding group.

"Hey, Katya, since you're studying photography and need a project, how about nude shots on horseback?" Heidi turned in her saddle. "Any volunteers? We need 12, one for each month on the calendar, just like the ladies in the film, *The Calendar Girls*, except we're a little younger." There were only four people there at the time. No one volunteered. The promise of only taking discreet photos didn't even entice them. Heidi didn't want to get photographed either, so she was relieved no one agreed and let the subject drop. The lesson ended soon after. They groomed their horses, put the equipment back in the tack room, and released the animals into a nearby field.

Heidi went home buzzing with energy. She started rice bubbling in the designated electric cooker, then tucked a hearty stew into the crockpot for later. With her kitchen duties humming along, she headed outside to dig fence post holes for the family's vegetable garden. When complete, it would be a neat twenty square foot plot with six separate planting areas according to her roughly drawn sketches. She thought she was alone until one of their miniature horses tiptoed up behind her like a nosy little shadow. He sniffed and pawed at the freshly dug earth, snorting and sneezing, making the task even more challenging.

As if on cue, Heidi's children arrived home from school, eager to dig instead of doing their homework. Their enthusiastic desire to help was appreciated, but the post holes would take days to complete with all the help. Heidi didn't have the patience to allow animals or humans to get further involved.

She sent the children inside, but she soon found that they had gotten themselves into mischief. They had helped themselves to the partially cooked rice and had finished it before the stew was even close to being ready. Drops of rice were scattered across their math papers on the kitchen table, but no computations had been completed. As the absurdity of the situation sank in, she had to laugh. Before she could decide how to proceed, the doorbell rang.

Rushing to answer, Heidi discovered a neighbor on the doorstep with Jack. Their beloved Jack Russel terrier was filthy. He bounded into the house and started a full-blown argument with his littermate over a bone she was gnawing. Mud spattered everywhere. Heidi's twin sons tried to stop the argument and ended up just as dirty. The neighbor pointed out, while remaining on the doorstep, that she'd seen Jack digging in the yard. Heidi looked over the woman's shoulder. There was a trickling brook coming from the hole Jack dug that didn't belong there in the middle of a drought. The smell of wet earth was far more pleasant than a wet dog. Exploring together, the women figured out the water was coming from the wellhead.

After calling Walt at work, they decide to contact the plumber who had recently helped renovate the children's bathroom. Heidi and Walt used to do all their household renovations and repairs themselves, but it had become too much of a chore. Nevertheless, as soon as Walt got home, he hopped on his used John Deere tractor in their field and brought it around to the soggy front yard. He was proud of his tractor. At the time of purchase, it was a needless extravagance, but over the years it proved invaluable. While the entire family watched from the front porch, Walt dug a six-foot hole down to the source of the leak and propped boards inside to prevent the earth from collapsing inward.

Looking at his work, he said, "See, I put my skills to use. Aren't you glad I bought this marvelous piece of equipment?"

"Still no," Heidi puckered her lips. He leaned in and kissed them.

The plumbers eventually showed up after spending all day with an emergency on someone else's property. By the time the workers arrived, the remaining path to the house was saturated and looked like a gurgling Yellowstone geyser.

∽

Heidi thought the remainder of the day couldn't get any more chaotic. Inside the house, she touched a light switch on a lamp in the alcove by the kitchen. The bulb exploded and fell to pieces on the counter, surrounding her dad's Cadillac keychain. Facing his recent death continued to be difficult. She fished the keys out of the mess and hung them back on the hook. After cleaning up the counter, she made a note to herself to deal with the car in the days ahead. There was no use in ignoring the inevitable.

Frustrated, she muttered to herself, "I'm tired of all this. I just want some peace and quiet. Perhaps a little ironing will relax me." *Wrong answer, wrong answer!* She plugged in the iron, and the three computers in the next room over shut off with the overloaded fuse. Down the stairs she went, heading to the main fuse box. The basement smelled faintly of damp concrete. Halfway down, her son called out, "Mom, I dropped my airplane in the toilet by mistake."

She flipped the switch and headed back up. "Uh, uh. Was it really a mistake?"

"Um." He covered his eyes. "No. I wanted to see if it floated. And then I wondered where it would go and what the passengers would see."

"It would swirl around in circles and go through the dark pipes to a treatment plant with lots of other stuff." Heidi titled her head back and forth. Her neck cracked with each motion.

"Like what, Mommy?"

"Questions, questions." She sighed. "It's not a nice place. Everyone's wastewater goes there. It's dark and smelly."

"Like poo?" he asked.

"Yes, yes," Heidi replied. She marveled at how even gross topics fascinated her six-year-old boys.

She couldn't help but smile at this situation as it reminded her of another toilet incident—far worse—when a lightbulb went down the drain, flooded the floor, and Walt had to pull the toilet off its foundation to dislodge the culprit. At least this situation wasn't as catastrophic.

"All right, this is definitely a 'Calgon™ take me away' evening," Heidi mumbled. She mumbled so often these days that she wondered if only the walls were listening. She managed to smile regardless. Out from under the sink came the rubber gloves and bleach. Both items went into the toilet to rescue the airplane. As the plane was being rescued, the telephone rang four separate times. Each caller left a long message, which blared through the answering machine. Perhaps the next caller would ask if she'd rescued the airplane. At some point, amidst all of this, Walt was desperately trying to get the ride-on lawnmower tire repaired before the six-inch grass in the backyard could get one fraction taller. His toolbox kept getting emptier while he tried different techniques and mumbled unintelligible words. Somehow, the evening finally calmed down, and dinner—what was left of it—arrived magically on the table at the unusually late hour of nine o'clock in the evening. With a sigh of relief, she was glad to have survived another day.

Heidi woke up the next day, stretched, and smiled, wondering what adventures awaited her. She put a robe on, got out of bed, walked to the window, and looked out over the back of the property. The yard seemed to stretch on forever, with horses and people everywhere. Walt and Heidi were already prepared for the day. They headed outside to mingle with the visitors who had been there since dawn, setting up for a horse show along with a few vendors selling horse-related items. Somehow, everything had come together without Heidi lifting a finger—except to agree to the event. One of their guests, an old associate who had a penchant for over-the-top pleasantries, rushed over to greet her with a broad smile.

She said, "It's good to see you! Thank you so much for sponsoring this event. We'll be having one at our place next month. I hope you'll come with your clients."

Heidi nodded, thanked the woman, and walked away laughing quietly. *I would have thoroughly enjoyed giving the woman a piece of my mind, and not too gently, either. She was always so difficult to deal with when I first got involved with horses. From one day to the next, no one knew what kind of mood the woman would be in. Never mind, the day is glorious, and when everyone is gone, I will groom a horse and ride off into the woods.*

Heidi rolled over again in bed and realized the event was all a dream. The property was real, but it wasn't theirs. It was a place she and her friends had visited the week before. It was a decorator show house that belonged to another family. They had offered it to the local historical society and then it was decorated by designers at no cost to the owners. Tickets were purchased and the proceeds from them, as well as any items visitors chose to purchase at the event, went back into benefiting the historic sections in town. Heidi always thought she'd love to have an old-fashioned estate with horses, but only if there was staff to take care of things. She figured she would never have that much money and even if she did, the reality of such a place would be more than she would want. So instead, the place became a memory, along with a jar of strawberry preserves she had picked up that day.

She lay there with the faint scent of hay and leather lingering in her mind. The sunlight filtered through the curtains, reality nudging her into the current moment along with the smell of coffee. Walt had undoubtedly made a pot. Glancing at the clock, she almost jumped out of bed before realizing it was Saturday and the children would likely still be asleep and didn't need rousing for school. Walt, like all Saturdays, was probably sitting on the front porch enjoying the sun's warmth. It felt like it was too early to dive into the day's chores. Donning her robe, she went to the kitchen for a cup of coffee. A familiar glint of her dad's Cadillac keychain caught her attention.

The car. She'd put off the oil change for weeks, and now guilt mixed with the tangle of responsibility. His absence didn't change the car's needs. That car wasn't merely transportation, it was a piece of her dad, a link to memories as vivid as her dream. It smelled like him; like Old Spice™. She had to stop pretending nothing had changed. It was time to get dressed and take care of things.

Driving down the road in the Cadillac, Heidi could feel the weight of time pressing against her. The car, a gleaming pearl white, still had the unmistakable smell of leather, just like when her father, Nathan, had first brought it home over a decade ago. It was the kind of car that turned heads—not because of its luxury, but because of the memories that were undoubtedly attached to it. Every dent, every scratch carried a story, and Heidi wasn't ready to let those stories go just yet.

The last time the car had an oil change was two years and 2000 miles ago. The car had a fine layer of dust covering its surface after being unused and garage-kept for quite some time. She rehearsed her explanation in her head as if the mechanic would judge her for not bringing it in sooner. After all, her dad had gone to the same mom and pop shop for decades. The 45-minute drive with her dad's classical music playing in the background soothed her soul.

As Heidi pulled into the shop, the mechanic raised an eyebrow and came up to her window to say hello. "I know this car." He circled what Heidi considered an old relic, and said, "Eleven years old and still looking fine. Your dad hasn't been in for a while."

"Well, no. Um, no, he recently passed away."

"I'm sorry. Such a gentleman." He stepped back, and Heidi got out of the car.

She smiled, remembering how meticulous her dad had been about its upkeep. "He used to say, a car's not just a machine, it's part of the family."

The mechanic was so impressed with the condition of the vehicle that he said, "if you ever want to sell the car, let me know." His voice trailed off as he inspected the tires.

Heidi chuckled. "Sell the car? It contains memories of both my parents throughout the years."

"Of course, of course. Let me know if you change your mind."

"Well, it's already going to a family friend."

"Good, good. I'll make sure everything is shipshape. Unless there's something unexpected, it should be ready in an hour. Go on into the waiting room while I change the oil and look it over."

Right after the car was worked on and various mechanical checks were conducted, Heidi paid the bill and received a coupon for three dollars off the automatic car wash next door. Normally, she preferred going to the do-it-yourself car wash, where she could take her time spraying the soap, scrubbing the tires, and making sure every inch of her car was gleaming. But today, she decided to take a trip down memory lane.

She drove the car up to the entrance, used the coupon, and pulled into the bay when the lights signaled her to move forward. Once in place, the machine came to life and giant blue brushes began doing their job. Soap suds splattered against the windows, and the water jets roared to life. The familiar scent of detergent filled the air. Heidi sat back and let herself relax, watching the rhythmic movement of the equipment. But then something unexpected happened. A lump formed in her throat, and before she could stop herself, a tear slipped down her cheek. She squeezed her eyes shut, caught off guard by the sudden rush of emotions.

Memories came flooding back, as vivid as if they had just

occurred yesterday. She and her dad, Nathan, used to go through a car wash like this all the time. It was their little tradition. He had loved the car wash. He'd lean back in his seat, close his eyes, and smile like a contented child. To most people, it was a mundane chore, but for them, it was an event. Afterward, they would drive out, and he'd run a towel over the roof and mirrors to make sure every drop of water was gone.

Heidi hadn't thought about these memories in years. Life had gotten too busy between work, relationships with others, and the simple passage of time. It had been easy to forget small but important rituals. Nathan had been gone for three years. She rarely allowed herself to dwell on his absence. But sitting there, in the midst of the whooshing brushes and the mechanical hum of the car wash, the weight of it settled in. Her dad was gone from this world, but at that moment she could feel his presence as clearly as if he were sitting in the passenger seat beside her while she watched soap bubbles.

When the car emerged from the wash, the sun hitting the now-gleaming paint, Heidi pulled over to the side. She sat for a moment, letting the car idle, and wiped her eyes with the back of her hand. It was strange how something so small could bring such an intense wave of emotions to the surface. But isn't that how life works? The little things are often the ones that leave the biggest impact.

With a deep breath, she stepped out of the Cadillac and grabbed a towel from the trunk. Just like her dad used to do, she carefully wiped down the mirrors and roof, making sure every drop of water was gone. It felt right, finishing a ritual that they had started so many years ago.

Heidi drove away, the Cadillac humming smoothly beneath her. Glancing in the rear-view mirror, the world looked different, brighter. A memory, hidden, had washed over her when she least expected. And just like that, her dad was with her again.

Pulling the Cadillac into the driveway took Heidi back to Walt and their children. Through the front window, she could see her daughter sprawled out on the couch, halfheartedly doing her home-work. The last few days had been a blur of mishaps. However, after sitting in the car remembering her dad, she realized those messy, unpredictable moments would one day be the stories their own children would carry with them.

She stepped inside the house, the faint smell of yesterday's meals lingering in the air, and called out, "What's the plan for din-ner, chef?"

Her daughter rolled her eyes and grinned. "That's your job, Mom. I'm just here for moral support. Sorry, how about pizza?"

Laughing, Heidi joined her on the couch, pulling her textbook off to the side. "You know," she said, "when I was a kid, your grandpa used to say life's little messes are where the best memories come from. He would have loved to be in the midst of our little disasters."

Her daughter smirked. "I suppose, but he didn't come here much."

"Well, he was really old when you all were old enough to know what he was like."

"I bet he was pretty cool when he was younger."

"He was," Heidi said, ruffling her hair. "And someday, you'll tell your kids all about how your mom managed to blow out the power and deal with a broken well all in one day."

"Ugh, children. I can't imagine. Well, if I do, I hope they don't ask me for cooking tips."

As they laughed together, Heidi felt the weight of the last few days lift. Life's chaos wasn't just something to endure; it was the thread tying generations together. And maybe, just maybe, amidst the mishaps, she could paint the day with memories worth keeping.

DRIVING THE DISTANCE

Since her father's death, Heidi had become busier than she'd ever been in her life. Her calendar was full, and it seemed like there wasn't another spot to write another word in the allotted squares most days. Driving the children to soccer practice, scouting events, gymnastics and horseback riding lessons felt like an unending carousel. It was all part of her job. Her husband, Walt, brought in the money to keep the family going and was primarily involved with their children's schooling. Now, Heidi had her mother to care for as well in a town an hour away. Often, she felt overwhelmed. Her only free time was on Friday mornings. In those hours, she relaxed with her draft horse while they rode through the woods. His robust and steady disposition, along with the rhythmic movement of his hooves, seemed to follow along with her heartbeat and helped settle her soul.

As they forged through narrow trails. Heidi couldn't help but reflect on the twists and turns of her own life. She thought of the dark places, the corners of her mind where sadness waited to pounce, and wondered if she would ever truly escape them. The chill in the air wrapped around her, creeping into her bones. She took a deep breath of the autumn air, catching the scent of the peaty leaves that lay on the ground, a sharp contrast to the acrid smells of her mother's old age, and proceeded down the trail.

When they arrived at a river crossing, the horse halted, ears flicking back. The water trickled over smooth stones in front of them, mirroring the stream of thoughts that flowed through Heidi's mind—each bend in the river, a metaphor for the obstacles she faced. This wasn't like him. His usual confidence seemed to falter, and she could feel the tension in his warm body. The water trickled over and around smooth stones. Upon closer inspection, Heidi saw a cluster of thick branches twisted among the rocks, creating a silhouette that resembled a trapped creature. The shape tugged at her own fears, like an echo of the grief she'd been trying to bury. No wonder her trusted friend refused to forge through the otherwise placid waters.

With gentle encouragement, he moved forward. On the other side of the river, they rode for another half hour, but the peace Heidi sought on this particular day was elusive. The woods, usually her refuge, felt more like a mirror, reflecting back her unrest.

Sitting in the car after the ride, Heidi let out a long breath. She could feel her responsibilities waiting for her, like a storm gathering on the horizon. As she shifted the car's gear into reverse, the barn manager approached the window to discuss the upcoming horse show. Distracted by the conversation, the car started to roll backward. Before Heidi could respond—the thud came.

For a split second, the world narrowed, and her vision blurring with panic. The first thought; *oh my God, have I run into a horse or a person?* She threw the gear back into 'park' and jumped out with her breath catching in her chest. Relief washed over her as she saw the damage was to a car and not a person; she'd bumped the side of the barn manager's car. The dent was barely visible, but Heidi's apologies spilled out in torrents. Each word felt like an attempt to wipe away her carelessness, as if by saying 'sorry' enough, she could erase the stress that clung to her. The barn manager decided not to file an insurance claim, and they went their separate ways.

Heidi resumed her usual duties. Among other things, she drove her mother to a heart specialist. With every step toward the door of the doctor's office, her mother moved more slowly. Inside the waiting room's fluorescent lights buzzed overhead, and antiseptic smells closed in on Heidi. After checking in at the reception desk, they sat on the cushions of stiff-backed chairs. The examination took place. The diagnosis; mitral valve prolapse or MVP. To prevent more damage, blood pressure and cholesterol medication were prescribed, but surgery was not an option for a ninety-two-year-old woman. After leaving the office in a despondent mood, they hobbled back to the car for the ride down River Road. To cheer them both up, Heidi drove to Austin Orlando's barn to see her Arabian horse.

Struggling out of the car and over to the sleek, grey horse standing at the fence line brought a smile to her mother's face. A smile that hadn't appeared in months. Tears welled up in Heidi's eyes. To conceal them, she left her mother and went into the barn to get a few treats to feed the horse. Upon returning, she put a molasses biscuit in her mother's open, shaking palm. He took it gingerly while Heidi stroked his muzzle. Her mother hadn't been near a horse in years, except in dreams, and this moment felt precious.

The moment was shattered by the sharp ring of Heidi's cell phone. Walt, on the other end of the line, began speaking in a rapid, clipped tone. His otherwise routine trip that morning down Route 29, created in honor of the local 29th Infantry of WWII, had almost ended in disaster. Their old silver truck and matching steel horse trailer they called the 'iron lung,' due to its bulky mass, had plowed through a red light.

While she waited for the rest of his story to unfold, her mind flashed to the massive steel trailer, imagining it careening down the road. Her chest tightened, the fear raw and palpable. The familiar pressure built in her chest. He said he couldn't stop because the power brakes had failed when he pressed the brake pedal uselessly to the floor and stayed there. He yanked the steering wheel to the right and cranked the emergency brake. Not exactly on two wheels, but close, he managed to turn into the adjacent parking lot in Burtonsville and come to a rolling stop near the Amish Market.

The therapy pony Walt was trying to transport appeared unscathed. The children, who'd come along for the ride, were also fine, but a little overexcited. That morning, Heidi had asked him to drive their therapy pony to Towson, near the University of Maryland, to be the guest of honor at a child's birthday party at the request of the child's wheelchair-bound grandmother. This was a far better option than the last time Mrs. Phillips had asked for such a service at her own home, six months before. On that occasion, it didn't go well. There, Heidi had walked the pony over to the house. Mrs. Phillips was moving around the yard with her new motorized wheelchair. At that time, the woman had another grandchild in her lap, who must have been about a year old. Heidi walked up with the pony, and in the excitement of the moment, the wheelchair started to tip sideways. With unexpected strength and determination, Heidi pushed the heavy chair, full of its precious cargo, back into an upright position. The pony only danced in place during the ordeal, which was a blessing, as it could have pulled away or reared and injured them all.

Walt wanted Heidi to struggle through twenty-five miles of rush-hour traffic without delay. The onboard GPS navigation system indicated it would be at least a two-hour journey rather than the usual forty-five minutes.

Heidi pulled at her lips with one hand while the other tightened on the steering wheel, her mind racing through the logistics of traffic, timing, and her family's needs. She said, "I'm not driving a car that can tow the trailer. Call Bob. He's a good neighbor. It's a fifteen-minute drive from his place. He has a truck." She heard Walt let out a long breath on the other end of the line. "Walt, I'm sorry. I'll phone Mrs. Phillips and let her know what's going on." Heidi's voice was tighter than she intended. Everything was piling up, threatening to drown her.

Heidi knew Walt wanted her to come to the rescue specifically because if it inconvenienced her mother, all the better. They all knew her mother had no love for her daughter's choice in husbands. After all, he had been doing Heidi a favor by taking on a task she was supposed to be doing. The horses were her passion, not his.

Heidi pacified him by saying, "if you or the kids were injured, I'd come right away, even if it meant hauling my mother along to the scene."

He conceded, indicating that it wasn't necessary. He'd call Bob. Nevertheless, Heidi was quite rattled and would not feel any better until she got home. After all their married years, she was still very much in love with him. When they got into arguments, she felt like cracker crumbs on the floor while worrying he would leave her. Logically, Heidi knew this was ridiculous, but sometimes she lost sight of reality and her insecurities took over. To compound her angst, her mother wrongfully acted as if he didn't exist while demanding constant attention from Heidi. This had been going on for two decades since Walt had whisked her away. With trepidation, Heidi drove her mother home and dropped her off with the housekeeper. She sat in the car for a moment longer, realizing her mother was oblivious to the storm rising within Heidi's chest. Between her mother's diagnosis of mitral prolapse and the dangerous event on Route 29, she could barely control the flood of tears threatening to erupt from her eyes. Her father's recent passing was enough in and of itself to deal with. She had enough to do raising children without the stress of her mother's troubles. With steadfast resolve, she held herself together and headed down the highway to Walt and their children.

Life…so it goes. Events kept moving forward whether Heidi was ready or not.

THE MOMENT SHE LET GO

Heidi sat on her pony's bare back, feeling the wiry tension of his muscles beneath her. The summer air was thick, as if it had been holding its breath, anticipating the chaos about to unfold. Up the hill they went. The pony moved faster and faster to avoid his pain, just as she began to experience her own. Heidi knew he had a cancerous sore on his belly, but she still decided to ride. The guilt gnawed at the edge of her conscience, but she ignored it, too consumed by her own needs. Running seemed like a cure for both of them. How could her father be dead? For the first time, she truly understood the fragility of life—death was inevitable. She had been strong and brave when he was alive and now felt afraid of everyday family events.

The pony crested the hill and began to turn sharply to the right as Heidi leaned toward the left. She knew what would happen and didn't care. The world tilted; sky and earth blurred together in a confused swirl. Her eyes closed. Gravity pulled her down, but it felt almost merciful, as though surrendering to the hard, cold, hellish ground was a small relief from the weight she carried within. Her life had become emotionally unbearable. In those split seconds, she didn't think of anyone—not her children, not her husband, not anyone. The overwhelming numbness had created a void, swallowing all the love she had always felt but couldn't reach. She wanted the horrible, soul-numbing oblivion to swallow her grief.

While she was unconscious, she dreamed about a dog. His fur shimmered, and his eyes gleamed with ancient wisdom. He said it wasn't her time to leave the earthly realm. It was time to grasp hold of life's wonders, of family, of friends, and of undiscovered things to come. It was not time to die.

When she woke, an untold number of minutes had passed. The sky glared down at her with perceived disapproval, and she realized how small and exposed she really was. How small compared to the magnificent cloudless sky. The pony chomped lazily at the grass, as if her tumble meant nothing to him—a reminder of how insignificant her problems must be in the grand scheme of things. She only remembered closing her eyes and falling, not hitting the hard, unyielding ground. Does God protect people this way before they die? She wondered if that final moment of grace was a whispered promise, a tender secret shared between the living and the dead. Maybe people and animals don't feel pain as they leave this world for the parallel universe people call heaven.

Heidi scolded herself for being so selfish; she didn't really want to die. The sharp bite of shame cut deeper than the growing pain in her neck. Her family needed her, and she was valued. The thought of her children's laughter echoed in her mind, a reminder of the life she was meant to hold on to. She lay on the ground, motionless. The ache in her neck was beginning to radiate down her back. For an instant, she imagined never walking again after the traumatic landing, and what the consequences to herself and family would be. A life in a wheelchair. There was no one around to pick her up. She'd deliberately left her cell phone in the house. It was as though she had set the stage for her own disaster and redemption. She had to get up on her own, both in body and soul. She rolled over, supporting her head with her hands, and sat upright.

Each movement sent a flare of pain through her spine, but she gritted her teeth and forced herself to keep going. Walking up the hill and into the house, she found an ice pack in the freezer and applied it to the back of her neck. She thought about the dog and wondered who he represented. Why had she allowed herself to fall off her pony? Her life was full of blessings, yet she felt overwhelmed.

She was wide awake in her pain and vowed to never shy away from life's heartaches again. Even so, the dog's words had frightened her. Messages? Words? Dogs can't talk. The visions must have been nothing more than an unconscious delusion. Or was it? Somewhere deep inside her, a flicker of doubt mingled with the hope that maybe—maybe—the dog was right. All beings are reincarnated. The prospect presented an alternative to her Christian upbringing. While she sat in the kitchen, she decided that this life was still worth living.

AN EQUESTRIAN JOURNEY

The purchase was a long time in coming. Finally able to pursue her own interests, Heidi took the leap and bought a turnkey equestrian business. She had always intended to go back to work in an office somewhere locally once her youngest began first grade, but nothing had turned out the way she had planned. It was impossible for her to juggle holding down a job and raising her children while caring for her elderly parents as long as they lived an hour away and needed her. Now that her parents had passed, and her children were older, it was time to take a leap of faith.

Her friend Donna asked her to explain her long history with horses. Initially, Heidi hesitated, since the answer would take some time to explain. However, it made sense. Donna needed as much background information as possible if they were going to run a horse farm together. Part of Donna's job would involve helping the clients gain confidence in their combined qualifications. Heidi excelled in one-on-one conversations but firmly believed her presence at the introductory meeting would not benefit the business. Her heightened anxiety during past speaking engagements in crowded rooms made her feel stilted and awkward, even with a podium to shield her. She feared being judged unfairly and had no desire to talk herself out of a corner. Donna had no such concerns. If any concerns arose, Donna could easily address them. She had a talent for engaging a crowd and achieving successful outcomes. During the client meetings, Donna would effectively convey her confidence in Heidi as the new owner of the business.

Heidi decided meeting at the local park overlooking the lake would be a relaxing setting. They agreed to meet the following Monday. As she sat on a bench waiting for Donna with her coffee, she was distracted by birds feasting on sunflower seeds a passerby had sprinkled on the path. The pleasant scene created a welcome diversion from the swirling thoughts in her mind. She became so absorbed that she nearly catapulted off the bench when Donna greeted her. Thankfully, the coffee cup was nearly empty. They shared a giggle and settled down, side by side, on the bench.

Donna got right down to business. "How did you get involved with horses in the first place?"

"Well, it all started when I was a kid. My parents got a pair of rabbits for me to take care of in our backyard."

"Rabbits to horses, that's quite a leap!"

Heidi laughed. "Yeah, it was. At an elementary school fair, I rode a pony for the first time wearing a ridiculous floral dress and an Easter bonnet."

"Wow! The same thing happened to me, but at a county fair without the fancy outfit. Sounds like the pony rides hooked us both."

"Yep. I was obsessed. Lessons, camps, anything to do with horses."

Ever since that first ride, Heidi's parents, Gwen and Nathan, had done what they could to support Heidi's interest in horses. It was a life she might never have experienced if she hadn't been adopted by the American couple when they found her in a German nunnery at two months old. A memory she never held consciously. Although well loved, some people say that an adopted child experiences a kind of disconnection throughout their entire lives that causes various levels of unexplainable insecurities. Perhaps this fact, or Gwen's lack of natural parenting skills, created Heidi's fear of being judged along with the resulting anxieties. She didn't completely understand her family, but she understood the power of healing that horses could bring to those around them.

Many times over the years, the family attended steeplechases in Middleburg, Virginia. At these events, they either had a tailgate picnic while watching the horses and jockeys thunder across a grass racetrack, or made their way to someone's house to celebrate afterward. Nathan always dressed in a suit with a bow tie and a cap on his head. Gwen and Heidi wore long dresses with their hat brims filled with flowers and feathers. Fashion surrounded every aspect of their lives. Gwen insisted on this point.

When Heidi turned eleven, Gwen signed her up for lessons at an equestrian center. Heidi's required dress included a velvet helmet, a striped button-down shirt fastened up at the neck with a cylindrical pearl pin, breeches, and high boots. Two years later, her enthusiasm for anything horse-related, combined with a dose of longing and pleading, landed her in a week-long horse adventure at Camp Waredoca, followed by a family vacation to a dude ranch in Colorado and many trips to Mackinac Island, Michigan. Horses, horses, and more horses.

"Donna," Heidi said. "Hope this is clear?"

"Mmm, yes," came the response. Her plaited blonde braids bounced on her shoulders when she moved her chin up and down in rapid succession. Donna had recently visited Jamaica, and the plaiting had been a treat. She leaned in. "What's your favorite part of Mackinac?"

"My mother's family has a long history with Mackinac. Whenever we vacationed there, Dad drove because Mom was afraid of flying."

"That's a long drive from here," Donna interjected.

"Yes—I sat in the front seat with Dad. Mom always sat in the back. I'm not sure why I brought that up." Heidi, who was inherently open and frank during conversations, now wondered if she was making herself vulnerable by telling Donna too much. And this wasn't related to horses. But she hadn't quite gotten over her mother's death and got stuck on extraneous facts. Nevertheless, she continued. "Mom didn't like the windshield so close to her face if we were in an accident. A new law required people to wear seatbelts in the front seats. Mom said she didn't like being held hostage by the contraptions."

Donna uttered a *tsk* sound similar to what one might use to encourage a horse to move forward. "Instead, she sacrificed you to the possible perils of the front seat. Poor kid."

"Yeah, right, I know. Anyway, the drive took forever. We spent one night at a hotel. One time, the only available place in town, picked at the last minute, wasn't ideal for Mom. It was a four-star, but she was less than thrilled. She slept in a chair. In retrospect, I think it had to do with her constant fear of germs in unfamiliar places. I was mortified by her behavior and subsequent ranting, even though no one other than Dad and me heard her."

"Germs? Really?" Donna drew out the words. "Thank God you didn't absorb that phobia."

"Her experience with the Spanish flu haunted her. Millions died in the early 1900s, including her mother. The extreme isolation and high death toll left a lasting impression. I am amazed she didn't have trouble helping soldiers in hospitals during WWII."

"Probably because they were wounded, not sick." Donna rubbed her temples. "I hope this story gets lighter."

"Sorry. I should probably get some counseling if I can't stop talking about my mother and her neuroses, but I always wondered if it was her erratic behavior that drew me to the steady and seemingly uncomplicated love of horses.

"During the drive to Mackinac, the first day was pretty dull on the major interstates. I'd search for license plates from every state and write them down in chronological order. I tried everything to keep from going stir-crazy. By the second day, we were on a long, narrow road with evergreen trees on either side. I'd stare out the window, counting them until my eyes got tired and I fell asleep."

"And Mackinac? I don't know anything about it. Did you drive straight onto the island?"

"No, there's a passenger ferry."

"What about getting around without a car?"

"Bikes and horses are the primary modes of transportation. Oh, and your feet. The only vehicles on the island are emergency types." Heidi considered the stark contrast between the cool temperature of the Great Lakes in June and the intense heat near the man-made lake where they were sitting. The ferry ride across to the island had always been chilly, with the wind blowing through her hair and tossing it across her face.

"I stayed with my older cousins at a B&B in the center of the island called The Inn at Stonecliffe. My parents slept at the Iroquois Hotel in town. No one bunked at the family home on the Bluff."

"Why did everyone split up?"

"No idea. Maybe a family secret. Could have been a space issue. Back to Stonecliffe. My cousins and I had our own rooms, and being without our parents around was fun. We were all there for a family wedding. Embarrassing—I can't remember who was getting married. At night, when there's nothing more than a crescent moon in the sky, the place gets really dark. It's haunted, I think. The spirits didn't bother me.

"I rode with some of my older cousins on hired horses from the local stable. They also had carriages. I explored the island with my parents in one of them on a different day. I loved it all."

"And the ranch?"

"It was totally different. No Great Lakes, just open plains." Heidi sneezed. "We rode twice a day in the mountains, had dances and bonfires at night, played games, and slept in cabins. I've never been so relaxed about anything."

"Sounds wonderful," Donna said. "Anything else?"

"Well, after that, I got distracted by other life events. I didn't ride again until Walt and I had our own children—four of them.

When the twins were eight-years-old, I drove by a horse facility multiple times a week, going back and forth to the kid's soccer practices. I talked so much about horses that Walt suggested I take lessons again.

"At first, I just rode the school horses, but after about a year, I leased a horse to see what it would be like to own one without the responsibilities. Gordo was slow and steady and needed a lot of encouragement to move forward. The barn used English saddles, and I think he was accustomed to Western types. He had the longest droopy neck I'd ever seen. It's amazing I never fell over his shoulders. As hard as I tried, I could never coax him into changing his posture.

"While I had Gordo, I tried to take very good care of him, but at one point the owner of the barn got angry at me for cleaning every bit of him, including his sheath even though a vet had taught me how to clean his privates properly. I had never seen that side of her until I started leasing. She was a very competent instructor who not only ran the facility but also worked with draft horses pulling carriages in the city. When I apologized for ending the lease with Gordo, she said, 'I do not need your pity.' I never understood what she meant. Right about then, it seemed like shopping for my own horse became very appealing. I enlisted Melisa, the children's instructor, to help.

"Melisa drove me out to another farm. When we got there, there were a number of horses being taken care of by a crippled 80-year-old woman. She wanted people to take her horses on a trial basis and pay later if they decided to keep them. I had my eye on Chester.

"From the ground, Chester looked sound, but Melisa advised me not to be the first to ride him. I didn't get the chance for quite some time. A month later, Melisa brought him to the barn and half-leased him to a student at the facility. Chester was a little wild and energetic, but he eventually calmed down and became quite responsive to commands. After about a month, Melisa offered me the other half of his lease. Once the teenager's lease ended, I decided to buy him, even though his pre-purchase exam mentioned some arthritis. Melisa worked out a purchase agreement with the older woman. With the swipe of a pen, he was mine."

"You must have been thrilled." Donna piped in.

"I was," Heidi said. "He taught me a lot about riding and equine healthcare. I think that's good information for the client meeting."

"Yes, I'll add it to my mental list," Donna said. "Oh, and your time at the local horse rescue facility."

"That certainly means something," Heidi said.

"No doubt. Anyway, go on about Chester."

"For the most part, I really enjoyed my time with him. Our first mishap surprised me. I was sitting in the saddle, asking Melisa for clarification about something she was teaching us while Chester stood still. Her dog liked to pick up things and toss them around. He'd often grab the string on a bale of hay, a lead-rope, or anything that would fit in his mouth and drag it around. On that occasion, he picked up an orange cone. Chester must have been dozing. He woke up, moved forward, and veered left and right. I was unprepared—shifted sideways off the saddle—and landed on my back. I looked up with my helmet askew, and Melisa was standing over me. She said I blacked out. I'd gotten the wind knocked out of me and damaged a rib." Remembering, Heidi rubbed her head and rib. "Concussion time. I recovered without any apparent lasting effects."

"You're tough," Donna replied.

"Not really. For the next year or so, we rode beautifully together without any mishaps. We have to make sure we have a helmet requirement for all our clients. When I bought the place, I noticed some of the riders weren't wearing them."

༄

The story continued. Heidi wanted more experience with caring for horses, which meant working closely with the vet, local farm stores, and area horse facilities. With Melisa's help and Walt's involvement, they found a way to have horses at home. Walt assembled a crew, built a small barn, and enclosed the surrounding acreage with post and rail oak fencing. When the task was complete, Melisa delivered two ponies from a charitable organization.

One of the ponies' roles was to have babies for the program. When they grew up, they became companions for children with disabilities. The ponies would either live with a disabled child or stay with a foster family and have supervised visits with the children.

A few months later, and unrelated to the program, Heidi's family bought three miniature horses in Florida and transported them up the coast. At the Georgia border, The Department of Agriculture had an inspection station. The authorities were puzzled about how the family had fit three horses into a trailer designed for two. The health papers explained the situation, but sense eventually prevailed when they walked around the exterior of the trailer and opened the side door to reveal the 'little darlings' who stood contentedly munching hay.

At home, Heidi and Walt's children were in charge of socializing the ponies and miniature horses to ensure they remained calm and obedient around people of all ages, as well as dogs. The whole family loved spending time with the miniature horses. Heidi was surprised by this because on a previous visit to the Land of the Little Horses in Pennsylvania, the children hadn't seemed interested. Back then, they could only observe the horses from a distance. Being able to interact with their own animals made all the difference. At one point, they had up to five miniatures in their yard—a newborn colt, a filly, and three adults—before working back down to three miniatures and two ponies.

༄

Chester changed. Heidi put her foot in the stirrup one morning and began swinging into the saddle. He moved forward at an alarming pace. She pulled herself up into the saddle, but wasn't able to fully seat herself before he moved forward abruptly. The stirrups swung left and right. She slid off his rear onto the ground in a muddy puddle with a thud as he ran away as if a monster was chasing him without any concern for her welfare. A staff member, who must have witnessed the event, rushed over and stared anxiously down at her.

"You all right?" the man asked.

"Yes, this is ridiculous." She tried to rub the mud off her hands, but to no avail. "Help me up."

"You sure you're okay?"

"Yes, yes."

He grabbed Heidi's hand and pulled her to her feet. Her legs were covered in muck. "I'm a resilient jellybean. For the most part." That wasn't entirely true. After the other falls from school horses, she'd torn muscles and pulled tendons, but over time, everything healed well enough. Fortunately, she'd never damaged her spine or brain. On this occasion, after recovering her senses and bringing Chester back to the barn, she removed his saddle and let him loose in the indoor arena. He lost his mind. He leaped and bucked like a wild stallion before jumping over the arena gate into the parking lot. The reason for his madness was unclear. Maybe it was time to stop riding him or give him some time off during the winter months.

Heidi considered replacing Chester with another horse in the spring, but in the meantime, she needed someone who had experience with unpredictable horses. Donna came to mind, but she was too tall for him, so Heidi abandoned the idea. Her plans to sell him were disrupted by a new issue; Chester developed a mysterious ailment. A swollen area with several wart-like bumps appeared on his sheath near his rear legs. Initially, Heidi suspected he'd been stung by a bee or a spider. Nevertheless, she telephoned the vet, and he seemed similarly unconcerned.

Several days later, Chester's belly emitted a particularly rotten smell. The vet was called. He sedated Chester and performed a thorough sheath cleaning to remove the infected debris clinging to his skin. A ten-day course of antibiotics followed. The treatment only offered temporary relief, as the putrid odor returned a few weeks later. Another vet visit revealed more nodules.

"How did this happen so fast?" Heidi asked.

"There's no way to know. I'm sorry," the vet replied. "I'll take a skin sample to the lab. Since Christmas is around the corner, getting results will take longer than usual."

"Oh," Heidi said and paused. The minute between the time she heard his words and the time she spoke again felt like an hour. "Maybe this explains why he runs off like a monster is chasing him?"

"Very possible. This ailment can be uncomfortable," the vet replied. "But it generally isn't a systemic issue."

Christmas and New Year's Day had come and gone by the time the results arrived. The report revealed that Chester had cancer. Heidi was presented with a number of options, but they were all bad. The first option—chemotherapy cream treatments, while hoping for a complete recovery. The second—partially amputating his sheath. The third—let the cancer run its course. The fourth—immediate euthanasia.

She chose chemotherapy treatments even though she'd have to inject a sedative into his neck before every application of the cream with impermeable gloves. The vet said the cream could never come in contact with Heidi's skin. The formula would make her quite ill. Would it really help Chester? Or would he be in perpetual pain? Was she doing this for him or for herself?

The vet showed her how to detach the needle from the syringe and "flick" the needle into the vial, then attach the syringe and extract the sedative. This technique worked for him, but Heidi preferred leaving the syringe in one piece while drawing out the liquid. The vet didn't object, as it was a personal preference. For the injection, Heidi tapped Chester's neck to distract him before putting the needle in with one jab and gradually pushing the plunger.

The injection worked to relax him the first few times, but then failed as he became aware of the cause of his pain. Heidi waited more days in between applications, but he wouldn't stand still. The vet returned, injected a powerful relaxant into a vein, and applied a stronger cream to expedite the process.

When Heidi hopped into her car and drove away from the barn, she was crying. She'd left the cream on the ledge in the stall in her haste to escape. Realizing her mistake, she rushed back, but it was gone. She raked through the shavings on the floor with shaking fingers and found nothing. More than the cream was lost; so were her illusions. Chester wouldn't fully recover, and it was time to stop the torturous treatment and let him rest. Moving him to their home to have the freedom to roam in their pasture until it was necessary to euthanize him seemed like the appropriate option. Even with the cancer, the vet said he could be ridden after his system settled down from the chemotherapy treatments.

Heidi tried to get Chester into a trailer for his five-mile ride home, but he didn't want anything to do with the trailer, as it creaked and groaned when he stepped inside. She gave up. A staff member got him on board using the smoke from the cigarette that hung from the edge of his mouth. The fumes calmed Chester. Heidi drove him home, and he backed out of the trailer like a pro.

The miniature horses, along with the two ponies, lived in a separate field from Chester. He was too large to share a space with them safely. Observing them through the fence kept him calm. Heidi desperately wanted to take him back to the public barn for her lessons with her friends. Even with an enticing mix of oats and sweet-smelling molasses sitting in a bucket at the front of the trailer, he refused to stay inside for more than a few minutes. Every time she started to close the back ramp, he would push his hindquarters against it. She had to let go of the ramp and step aside to avoid being crushed as he turned around and bolted into the field. After numerous similar episodes and much frustration, Heidi relented and enlisted helpers rather than taking up smoking cigarettes (after all that had worked before).

A neighbor came over with two musclebound friends. None of them smoked, so they used an old-fashioned technique with ropes. The first rope wove around Chester's head like a halter with a slip-knot. A second rope was under his tail and across his rump, with a person holding the rope on either end to encourage him to move forward instead of backward. The three men coaxed him onto the ramp while talking continuously. Chester strained his neck, stiffened his front legs, and fought against the ropes until he collapsed on the ground by the edge of the trailer's ramp. After he recovered, he walked into the trailer, and they secured the door. Heidi was devastated and vowed never to try such a method of coercion again. She wished she'd had connections to Monty Roberts, the horse whisperer, or Pat Parelli, the natural horsemanship handler, who both had more gentle approaches to persuading horses to follow human commands.

When Heidi tried to lead him into the trailer the next day, he refused even harder than before. The decision to recruit those men ended up being a complete, destructive waste of time. The end result, no off-site lessons. Heidi rode in the yard, but it was boring without someone to talk to or without a change of scenery. Up and down the slopes, over and over. The bank into the woods had too steep a pitch to climb. Private homes were all around, and there were no other riding areas within walking or trotting distance.

Chester soon developed an unexpected desire to take off at a full gallop through the field. This happened three times, once with their children and twice with Heidi. One child decided riding wasn't ever a good idea; the other dedicated herself to rigorous training off site. When Heidi fell off, she rolled over his shoulder, did a flip, landed on her back, and lost consciousness. Another concussion. Anyone else would have gone to the emergency room after the fall with the swelling that emerged around her neck, but Heidi nursed herself back to health. After the swelling subsided, the doctor said the X-ray showed signs of arthritis and no fractures. By the time her neck had stabilized, Melisa had moved to another farm. Heidi followed and started taking lessons again on school horses.

Some of the additions to their riding group posed interesting challenges. One person named Katya had a dog accompanying her 24/7. Heidi struggled to understand why Katya was allowed to bring the dog, since the barn didn't give any other clients the same privileges. After a while, she discovered the dog was a service animal and alerted Katya whenever someone came up behind her. Without him, her anxiety was overwhelming. He protected her from being knifed in the back again, as she had been in the city. Mentally, she realized this probably would never happen again, but emotionally she couldn't cope in public without her dog.

Then there was Judy, who often spoke at length about her hostility toward various people outside barn life, particularly her verbally demanding mother and husband. Her mother had suffered a stroke, yet was still able to speak, and every word seemed to cut into Judy. Her voice would quiver with exhaustion when she talked about both her mother and her husband needing constant attention. Then she'd complain about the horse she bought, who seemed to be very quiet and compliant with everyone but Judy. Her stress rolled right into the horse. He stomped his feet and twitched his neck as if he was being bothered by an invisible fly. The farrier would no longer shoe her horse because Judy constantly complained about his prices. To top it all off, she'd brag about her extensive experience with horses, but seemed to lack the basic knowledge and confidence one would expect. Judy's deep-seated anxiety was etched into her face with lines beyond her years. An anxiety that seemed to stretch back many years. Whether it started when her child died in a car accident and everyone blamed her, or before that, Heidi would never know. Heidi kept trying to help Judy relax, but she remained intensely hostile and resentful toward the world. While the barn served as a therapeutic space for many, this woman's stormy demeanor stifled her classmates. Everyone was expected to listen to her extremely depressing life without ever accepting anyone's advice. None of them knew if she was receiving professional help, but Heidi hoped she was. Judy's unrelenting negativity cast a shadow over the sanctuary they all cherished, leaving everyone on edge.

"You realize this is leading us back to where we started—owning a business and being able to handle all types of people?" Heidi sighed.

"Oh, yes. I completely understand where this is going," Donna said. "Hey, don't forget our old friend, Candice, who'd had even less experience than we do and owned a lesson barn. She was very successful."

"True. True. She *is*, and we'll be too. A psychology degree might be helpful." Heidi added, wiggling her shoulders to relax. "At least one member of our class can't be a troubled soul. This person has to be truly extraordinary and bring nothing but joy to this world. As a bonus—she absolutely must bring her darling children to the barn on occasion."

"Who?" Donna scowled. "Who are you talking about?"

Heidi tapped Donna's knee. "You, of course."

"Okay, okay. Thanks." Donna chuckled. "Refer to me in the third-person if that makes you happy."

"Thank you, I will." Heidi smiled. "Every day when we warm up for lessons, we talk and laugh. Everyone calls you a Velcro™ rider because you can stay on all the high-strung horses. No horse would dare go too fast, buck, or not listen to directional ques from your legs, words, or reins. I know you get attached to the difficult horses, and get down when they are shipped somewhere quickly because they can't be a school horse. Too much of a liability."

"Well," Donna said. "This is the way I see it. You just need to be confident and consistent in telling the horse who's boss. That's what I do. Horseback riding and driving a car are equally dangerous if you are not paying attention or not following the rules. Both sources of transportation are choices. You don't have to do either, but you ride because they are part of your spiritual survival."

"Right. You're so right." Heidi stared out at the lake.

♦

Heidi rode the school horses for several months while deciding when to start shopping for another horse. She found it impossible to get the sight of Chester receiving his injections, the last ones of his life, out of her mind. He bent down on his knees, then his haunches, and rolled onto his side. After one or two deep breaths, he left. His eyes glazed over and stilled. Heidi removed several strands from his tail for her photo album.

♦

It was Donna who pulled Heidi out of her despair. Donna started searching online and through local horse newspapers to find a horse to share. Heidi considered herself extremely lucky to have such a willing assistant. They were getting well educated, but not finding the right horse for an acceptable price. The search marked a turning point in their friendship when it started to evolve into a business relationship.

Heidi recalled walking into the barn office and talking to Manager Nan about what she wanted in a horse friend. A large, comfortable, safe one with splashes of color (a pinto) like Sandra's. He never nibbled on people and never pushed any man or horses around. His back was so level and plush it was like sitting on a couch in one's living room. He never swayed or shied away from anything. The rumor going around said he'd been a police horse. He was a draft breed, crossed with an unknown counterpart.

"That is a tall order and not likely to be fulfilled any time soon," Nan said. "In the meantime, think about this when you get on any horse. Riding is like a baker baking a cake. As the riders go along, they may make mistakes, but they find ways to correct the errors. Remember, every horse has issues."

"Profound. I'll work on being a better rider, but I still want to buy a horse that doesn't have a death sentence on the horizon." Heidi excused herself and strolled away to groom her school horse.

About a month later, after riding many horses at various people's facilities, Nan came through. A horse at a local event was standing in a pen with an attached sign that listed him for sale. His name was Cody, and he'd been a barrel racing horse. The price was right, so she bought him, figuring someone would buy him if Heidi and Donna didn't approve.

Back at the barn, Nan put him in quarantine to prevent any unknown maladies from transferring to the school or private horses. When Heidi arrived the next day, she was greeted by the couch she'd longed for. He was chestnut and white with a Shire's head and a heavy body that wasn't quite as trim as it should be but elegant, nonetheless. Happy bubbles and butterflies bounced around her stomach. If she were a bird, she would have taken off in flight with joy.

As time passed, everything was going along wonderfully with Cody. He didn't have troubles with trailers or anything else. Everyone in her class moved again to another new barn where the people were friendly. She moved Cody as well. They had found a place with many benefits that extended beyond riding. There was a community of like-minded horse-people. Like-minded as far as loving to ride or be around horses. No one ever talked about politics, religion, or anything beyond horses and their own children. Heidi rode Cody in the ring for lessons, and took him on rides through trails in the woods, and even rode him in the field without him taking off in a full, unrequested gallop. From then on, he was her loyal champion.

"Move forward," Donna paused and turned to face Heidi on the bench. "Now you've bought the farm. How? And why? Remember, I wasn't there when it was all arranged."

"No big deal, really. My daughter's employer mentioned it. I leapt at the opportunity, even though I realized I'd have to rearrange my life to make time for the extra work. As for the why—back when Chester died, I decided to do more for horses and the riders who love them. It just took me a while to get to this point."

"So, here we are. Full steam ahead. I'm ready to meet the clients."

"Thank you. I think we can give this horse business a shot and make a lot of kids happy."

THE FARMHOUSE GATHERING

Donna envisioned a weekly neighborhood meal beginning in the autumn months, where people would gather around the rustic wooden tables in the warm and inviting atmosphere of the cozy farmhouse. When she discussed the idea with the farm's owner, her boss and friend Heidi embraced the concept with enthusiasm.

"I love the idea, Donna!" Heidi said in her usual upbeat voice. "I'll get a list together of clients and neighbors."

The horse farm, bustling with activity, began with a few dozen horses for boarding, lessons, and summer camp. The horses ranged in size from ponies to draft horses. Each one was loved for their individual personality, like characters in a beloved novel. The community meals would certainly be a wonderful addition to the busy year-round activities that often included a weekend wedding or conference in the adjacent building.

Sitting at one of the tables, Donna couldn't have been happier while she organized the menu. The wooden table's surface felt smooth under her hand as she moved it back and forth, thinking of her past. These types of events were a regular occurrence in her teenage years when she helped her mother prepare and serve meals at the local church.

"Mom always said the secret ingredient to good food was love." Donna mused to herself, smiling.

Time passed quickly. Week after week, the house came alive on Wednesday evenings with the buzz of anticipation as familiar faces filled the rooms in the farmhouse. They sat around the tables or milled about the unfurnished living room, waiting for Donna's delicious home-cooked meals. The air was abuzz with conversations and filled with rich smells of garlic and onions infused with thyme. A perfect mix for the autumn sunset with the view out the picture window of the leaves turning in a variety of colors.

"Donna, this place is magical," said Mrs. Blake, a regular attendee. "Your meals remind me of home."

On this occasion, she'd chosen a beef stew recipe. It took a fair amount of time that morning to cut the beef into cubes along with the carrots, potatoes, and onions. Donna recalled Heidi laughing at her the first time the onion went under the knife because she always wore goggles to keep her eyes from tearing up.

"Still wearing those goggles, huh?" Heidi teased, peeking into the kitchen.

"You know it! They save my eyes," Donna replied with a grin.

She was a master chef in the kitchen, her culinary skills a magician's wand, turning simple ingredients into delightful dishes. People who had the means to help dropped a few dollars into the box by the stove, while those less fortunate expressed their gratitude with nods and a few words.

"Thank you, Donna. This means the world to me," said Mr. Jermone, one of the less fortunate guests.

Although Donna often relished the opportunity to try new recipes, her greatest pleasure was watching how the food brought people together. Community was everything, and running these dinners was, in a way, inevitable since the farm had an overstocked freezer, fridge, and pantry. All of it, the meat, the fruit, and the vegetables, had come straight from the family's land. What they couldn't consume, they either canned and sold or gave to local food kitchens to feed the homeless—ensuring nothing went to waste.

As Donna hurried over to the sink to fill a pitcher with water, outside the window she saw a set of shovels resting on the mound of soil. The hired hands were taking a break to drink something out of cans they'd removed from an adjacent cooler. It wouldn't be long before they finished burying Laddie and erected a headstone with his portrait embedded in the monument. The stone would serve as a touching tribute to a special friend and a permanent marker in the landscape of their memories. He was such a sweet miniature horse, a tiny titan who stole everyone's hearts.

"Laddie was a jewel," Heidi said softly, joining Donna at the window.

"He really was," Donna agreed, her voice thick with emotion.

Getting back to work, Donna hustled around in the kitchen, ladling up another batch of stew while monitoring the guests, some of whom she knew as clients from the horse barn and others she hadn't met before. She hoped the strangers had come with the clients and neighbors. One of them, a boy in a red plaid shirt, worried her. He wasn't eating—he was helping himself to a computer war game on the big-screen television in the alcove without bothering to ask permission.

"Excuse me, would you like some stew?" she asked, trying to engage him.

"Uh, sure. Thanks," he mumbled, barely looking up.

For reasons she couldn't explain, Donna wondered what he was up to. But with twenty or so guests roaming around the room, chatting with each other, she was too busy to keep an eye on him.

"Donna, the garden looks beautiful this year," Annie said, handing her a basket of fresh herbs.

"Thanks, Annie, we couldn't have done it without your help," Donna replied, squeezing Annie's hand. They had been long-term friends for more than twenty years. The farm was lucky to have Annie since she oversaw the care of the gardens and livestock. Just as they started talking, a knock on the door disrupted their conversation. The door cracked open. Someone announced that the job was completed, and the stone had been successfully positioned.

When Donna stepped outside, she noticed the man's gloves and boots were covered in dirt.

"Thank you," Donna said. "Please wait by the pond. I'll find someone to bring out your check."

A few minutes later, an unfamiliar man entered the house, walked up to Donna and flashed an FBI badge before introducing himself and handing over his card. "Ma'am, I'm Agent Collins."

Donna was taken aback and scowled rather fiercely at him. She couldn't, or maybe she could, imagine why the agent was there. Could it be about the young man? Or was it about the woman she'd also noticed sitting on a bench by the side of the house, who was chewing on her red fingernails while suspiciously tilting her head and glaring back and forth?

"What's this about?" Donna inquired.

"We are looking for a particular person who witnessed a murder. Someone said they came here," the agent readily replied. "Can we look around?"

Donna's heart picked up its pace. "I don't think we have a choice. Please be discreet. I don't want to upset any of our clients."

"Yes, ma'am. We'll be as unobtrusive as possible," Agent Collins assured her.

While the agents wandered around the room, Donna continued her kitchen duties in an effort to stay busy and out of the way. She washed a pan and looked out the window toward the pond where Heidi's husband was paying the hired hands for the burial. After Laddie's death, clients had reminisced about his antics around the arena. He loved to flex his stallion wiles when he was permitted to bolt around on his own. But perhaps he loved working with the young clients best while they held his lead rope and guided him over jumping poles of various heights. They only had a few miniatures on the farm amongst the twenty-five full-sized horses, but Laddie was special. His friend was an enormous draft horse with matching markings. Side-by-side, they looked like something out of a children's storybook.

The oven timer beeped. Annie beat Donna to it and rescued another apple pie with oven mitts. A smile spread across Donna's face; she loved the extra help. While the pies were cooling, they huddled together by the stove and ladled more stew into a simple serving dish that was nearly as old as the farm. Not all the guests had eaten their first portions since they'd been more interested in socializing, which also brought a smile to Donna's face. Building a community was the point, after all.

The young man in front of the television was still riveted to the screen. Donna carried a bowl of stew over to him. He looked up, but avoided her questions about his connection to the farm. Instead, his eyes nervously scanned the room and eventually locked onto the agent. He immediately appeared to understand who and what he was, even though the agent was dressed in jeans and a shirt like most of the other guests. How the young man knew or why he should be concerned wasn't clear, but he wasn't fooled. He devoured a few bites of stew before excusing himself and walking out the side door.

Following the young man to the door, Donna watched him veer around the 100-year-old oak trees and head toward the barn. The evasive tactic failed. One of the agents stopped and handcuffed him. Within five minutes, they got into the car, were joined by the remaining agent, and drove off without explanation to any of the curious onlookers who were in the process of leading their horses out of the barn for their next round of lessons, their feet harmonically clicking across the concrete. Close behind, a cow appeared and let out a long moo. The horse at the end of the line skittered in place and answered with a long neigh. There was no need to worry. It was the neighbor's cow, which often escaped from its field and roamed through the barn. Maybe it hoped to become a horse. The chickens often roamed the aisles as well.

Donna brought the agent's card out of her pocket, and her

mind raced back to the woman with the striking red nails. Eager to uncover another layer of the story, she discreetly circled around the side of the house. The woman was still there. Before forwarding the image to the FBI agent, she found Heidi in the barn.

"Do you recognize this woman?" She held up the phone.

"Well now, that is interesting." Heidi smiled. "She's the young man's grandmother."

"The one connected to the FBI?" Donna's eyes widened. "She didn't do anything when he was taken away."

"Yep." Heidi confirmed, her tone laced with irony. "Send the photo with a text message to the agent."

Donna complied; her curiosity piqued. "So, what's the deal?"

Her phone rang almost immediately.

"Ma'am, thank you for the photo." The agent's voice crackled through the phone. "The woman's already in our database. Her grandson's a witness to a heinous crime. We saw her sitting there, and we're keeping her under surveillance for the time being. We're certain she didn't suspect or see us take her grandson away."

Before Donna could ask any questions, the phone went dead.

BUDDY DOG

Heidi and Walt's life on the East Coast had been thrown into turmoil. Their family of six humans, two cats, one horse, and two dogs was rocketed into unavoidable despair, and some difficult choices. First, their largest canine friend died of stomach cancer, followed by Heidi's elderly mother of cancer. Once the dust had settled, they realized that the public schools their children attended weren't suitable. Rather than send them to a private school instead, they decided to move to another district. The decision wasn't well received by the children, which they voiced with loud expressions of discontent. In the middle of the school year, Walt and Heidi found an imperfect house they vowed to improve. The upheaval of these consecutive events threw the entire family into a state of depression. To lift everyone's spirits, they scanned the newspapers to find another large-breed dog to move into the new house with them.

Unbeknownst to the children, the following spring, Walt and Heidi drove to a home where puppies had been born three months before. One of them was sitting by a tree waiting while the others clamored around the human's legs. The mother was supposedly a long-haired fluffy Labrador, which Heidi had never heard of. The father was a blue Doberman. The puppies looked more like lanky legged lean Rottweilers with rust markings above their eyes and around their snouts, short black hair, and long wiry tails. Heidi was happy to see their ears were not cropped and their tails not docked because so many others in the community were. The dog's documentation stated a Doberman Lab mix. The Doberman designation would only be problematic if their new family lived in a corporate rental. Those and a few other breeds aren't permitted in such places. Hardly fair, but a fact. The list of potentially 'aggressive' dogs appeared to be growing. It seemed like each time a dog became unruly, those breeds were added to a list, to the detriment of all the other dogs who received proper training in loving homes.

Heidi chose the placid male puppy by the tree against Walt's advice or any written instructions she'd read about on how to pick a puppy. After all, they'd had dogs since 1984, and it was now 2006. She looked into his warm, chocolate-colored eyes and named him Buddy on the spot; no other choice would do. They paid the small fee to cover the sellers' expenses, slipped an old collar with a leash around Buddy's neck, and walked to the car with his documentation. He attempted to jump onto the passenger seat, but landed on the floor where he curled up at Heidi's feet. The temptation to pick him up and snuggle him in her lap overwhelmed her, except she knew it wasn't a good habit to start, since he would soon grow too large to hold comfortably. Cuddles would begin on a 'doggy bed' on the floor at home.

Before exposing Buddy to their other animals or children, they took him straight to the vet's office. There he crawled under Heidi's chair and stuck his snout between her hiking boots. She squeezed it ever so slightly and rubbed his ears to encourage the behavior. In the examination room, Dr. Short sat on the floor with Buddy rather than lifting him onto the cold metal table. A stethoscope to his lungs and heart, an ear canal check, a thermometer probe, a body check for bugs, a few vaccinations, and a drawn tube of blood. The available doggie treats were given liberally. All requirements passed. Next, a trip to the pet store where Buddy, with Heidi's hand signals and vocal commands, picked out a stuffed toy and a packet of dog treats. She knew he didn't actually understand, but training had to start from day one. He had to know who was boss, who was the leader of his pack. When they finally got back to the house, Buddy curled up, exhausted but content, in the front garden bed under the mature flowering peonies and fell asleep. It seemed as if he knew where he belonged.

They sat in chairs nearby and waited for the children to get off the bus and walk the half mile down the community lane. Needless to say, the children were quite surprised when they saw a puppy curled up in the yard. They hadn't expected to find a new dog and their dad at home from work on a Friday. They all huddled around Buddy with giggles and smiles while rubbing his ears and back. He licked them and wagged his tail.

It was time to bring out their three-year-old Jack Russell, who had an atypical elongated body that resembled a Dachshund. Heidi went inside and released him from his crate. He couldn't be trusted to run freely in the house when no one was home because he would chew up a window sill and soil the floor. Over time, she realized he felt most secure in the crate. Immediately after Heidi opened the back door to the house, Jack flew into the yard, circled Buddy, and sniffed at his new companion. Buddy took one look at the little squirt without reacting. He stood up, stretching, and even at three months old, he towered over the little dog. They moved around each other in a tight circle, which expanded into a full-out romping in the grass. The family declared the meeting a success.

∽

When Buddy was a year old, he had completed his training. His devotion to Heidi expanded beyond her to the entire family. He'd follow each person, shifting from one to the next, while they completed their morning routines for work and school. After everyone except Heidi had gone, he'd stick by her side. During the day, Heidi would go to work at her horse farm and take Buddy along. Each morning, Buddy's internal clock would go off, and he'd nudge Heidi's hand if she got distracted with washing dishes, sorting out the house, or reading the newspaper. Finally, she'd concede with a *let's go* command, and they headed out the side door with his tail wagging. He'd jump onto his seat in the back when the truck door was half open. Before driving off, Heidi called a staff member at the barn to let him know she was on the way, so he could judge when to feed Cody in his stall.

On the twelfth minute of the fifteen-minute drive, Buddy's internal clock would go off again. He'd stand and pace from one back window to the other, knowing they would soon arrive. The route and behavior were always the same. A half mile gravel road from the house to the main road, then to a county asphalt road, and finally to a short gravel driveway onto the farm through a squeaky, green cattle gate. As soon as Heidi opened the truck door and verbally released him, he'd take off into the barn. By the time she arrived next to him with a saddle and bridle, Cody was dribbling feed onto Buddy's head. It would roll off, and he'd catch the bits with his tongue. They both liked the sweet taste of the molasses in the feed. At least, that was her human opinion.

After a quick greeting to both dog and horse, she took the halter off the hook next to Cody's stall. While standing on her tiptoes, she slipped it over his head. Over the top of that, she added the bridle and tossed the reins over his head. This was their custom during workouts, but never for horse shows. Then, for Buddy, she attached a cotton braided lead rope onto the halter. Buddy grabbed the end of the rope in his mouth and ushered Cody into the outdoor arena. Sometimes it seemed like those two had a love affair going on. The animals appeared to have an understanding. Heidi released the lead rope and mounted the saddle. From then on, Cody obligingly obeyed Heidi's leg signals and the gentle use of the reins while moving ahead at the appropriate pace. These exercises were a far cry from his old life as a Western barrel racing horse. His workload had diminished, and he quickly adapted to an English saddle. It was as if he was on a never-ending vacation from his previous life. Whenever Buddy and Cody were together, Buddy followed several yards behind at a walk or run with his tongue hanging out and his ears bouncing.

༄

Heidi's daughter, Tessie, loved to hike at a brisk pace with Buddy. Undeterred, Heidi occasionally went along and worked-up a substantial sweat regardless of the temperature. She learned to bring along a change of clothes to freshen-up after hikes. Each time, Buddy would eagerly jump into the Subaru® for expeditions. Tessie charted out the route and guided them along narrow paths that traversed among rocks, protruding tree roots, and uneven ground levels.

The hike Heidi took with Buddy and Tessie at the Shenandoah National Park was the most memorable. The park's extensive network of 500 miles of trails, including a 101-mile section of the Appalachian Trail, was more than they wanted to take on. Instead, they planned to hike a small portion of a main branch with meager supplies in their backpacks. Tessie took her usual strides, stopped at every intersection, and waited for Heidi. The arrangement was satisfactory to the humans, but Buddy wasn't comfortable leaving one of them alone for long. His concern became quite apparent when he began running back and forth between them. After Buddy became rather winded and thirsty, they closed up ranks and walked together.

The two Camelbak™ water bladders they carried, along with a foldable bowl for Buddy, weren't quite enough. An hour into the three-hour loop, Tessie stopped at a stream. There, she pulled out the filtration kit from her backpack to purify and replenish their supply. It was easy. She only had to avoid a group of tadpoles and minnows living alongside a felled log. Tessie placed the tip of the tube in the water and pumped the handle back and forth while the water siphoned from the stream into the bladders.

Buddy's nose dipped in and out of the stream. On hot days, he loved to jump into the river near their house, and was often washed downstream a few hundred feet before bounding back up onto the bank. Thankfully, losing him in a river wasn't an issue on this trail, as the stream was strong enough to replenish their water supply, but not large enough to wash Buddy away. They prepared to move up the hill through the dense trees and underbrush that lay ahead on either side of the trail. The sun barely broke through the canopy of leaves.

At the top of the hill, a white-tailed deer emerged on the side of the path. Buddy, as was his custom, did not give chase without express permission, which neither human gave. Instead, Heidi leaned on his shoulders for support. She had fallen on another hike months before and injured her knee, but had recovered enough for hiking on level ground. With the command, 'wait', he would take one small step at a time as she did the same up the hill. With a tilt of his head, he kept an eye on the deer.

Further on, they came across a set of stairs resembling a ladder. Here, Tessie helped Buddy up the rungs, which was no small feat since he weighed close to eighty pounds. Tessie took on the task of putting his front feet on the second rung from the bottom and pushing his rump up towards the sky. He hopped forward while she pushed until the last rung, where he decided to catapult onto the path. The looped path Tessie had laid out went along for another three miles. By the time they arrived at the car, the sun was setting in hues of gold, yellow, and red.

It was a beautiful spring day with the massive thirty-foot trees opening their new leaves in every direction. The tulip poplars, with buds the size of baseballs, added an extra layer of natural beauty to the area. To enjoy the views and get some exercise, Heidi and Walt decided to stroll around the community. The stroll wasn't the usual grid of what one would find in a city. It required strolling through the woods at times rather than going around a four-cornered block. The four miles traversed through neighborhoods that flanked a long country road and a river. Some properties showed off manicured lawns, with boxwoods or azaleas outlining the grounds, whereas others were engulfed in underbrush, hiding homes in the rear of the lots.

On a plot of land on the other side of the river stood an abandoned building, once a tuberculosis sanatorium for African-Americans and later repurposed as a residence for the developmentally disabled, housing up to four hundred inhabitants. Its doors closed in 1985, and it slowly fell into disrepair. Some said it was haunted, but all they'd ever seen was graffiti, widespread vandalism, and news reports of fires. In its disrepair, trees grew inside and up through what was left of the roof. Windows were broken, asbestos tiles hung from the ceiling, chipped plaster lay strewn across the floor, and bathroom porcelain fixtures hung at odd angles on the walls. The forest had grown so dense that the old road with its washed-out bridge was impassable. Anyone wanting to explore the building had to cross the river on foot when the water levels were low. The powers-that-be finally decided to demolish it completely in 2013, which certainly saddened ghost hunters. But Heidi digressed by thinking of the tragic place instead of relaxing as they intended while walking along the route.

Even though it was a holiday weekend, there weren't many people socializing or gardening. The only exceptions were the two families who lived across the road from each other at a crossroads. Their similarities, perhaps, were limited to their location, but they both had barking dogs in their front yards. Presumably, they were discussing something between themselves in their language of yips and yaps while Buddy listened in. He remained silent and stood still next to Heidi. A long cord kept one dog in place, while the other dog roamed freely in front of an antique shop. The porch had a row of newly refinished pieces of furniture: a dresser, a rocking chair, a nightstand, and a kitchen table. Next to a detached garage, there were pieces of metal and wood intermixed with a wooden dresser partially sanded clean. The table instantly reminded Heidi of theirs back home. They'd had if for ten years after several lame attempts to strip off its yellow paint.

At first, they tried to stay closer to the tethered dog, but then decided to veer toward the unrestrained dog. This decision was reached after Heidi recalled being bitten by a tethered dog years before. The free dog from the antique shop advanced toward the road. She feared he might be hit by a passing vehicle. So, they decided to take their chances and headed over to the shop. As they approached, a man popped around a corner.

"Hello. Name's Bill. How can I help you?"

"Hello. I'm Heidi. This is Walt." She stroked Buddy's head. "Sorry for stirring up things."

"Dogs having their say," the man said in a husky voice. "Nothing to worry about."

"For years we've driven by here taking our kids to school. Figured it was time to stop by. We have a table we've been stripping yellow paint off forever. Can't seem to finish it."

"I can help if you want it done this year. Joan and I are planning to move to Sicily."

"Can we email you a photo and get an estimate?" Walt asked.

"Sure, sure." Bill handed him a business card.

"How's the refinishing done?"

"I either strip the finish off here or send it up to Baltimore for dipping. Then I scrape or sand it and put a new finish on."

"Okay, I'll send a photo of ours," Walt said, nodding.

In the ensuing silence, Heidi asked, "So, what's Sicily like?" Heidi asked during the ensuing lull in the conversation.

"It's below Italy and above Malta. Feels like living in the 1940s." Bill rubbed his bald head. "People are very direct and can be loud when they speak. No nonsense types. If you ask how they are, they'll tell you. I only start to worry when they talk softly and whisper. I hear foreigners can find them rude, but I like their approach to life. Funny thing is—the shops aren't always open when they say—which isn't direct at all. The same goes for buses. The time of arrival and the routes they take are inconsistent." He stopped talking and knelt down to pet Buddy and his own dog for a few minutes before standing up again. "There's a lot going on in Sicily. I could talk about it for hours."

"I've been to Rome, but never Sicily," Heidi said.

"Not the same at all." He paused as if recalling something significant. "Well, it is the best place on earth for us. We've made friends there over the years. We've saved most of the money we need for my long-term visa. Joan is a dual-citizen, so it'll be easy for her when she's healthy again." There it was, a possible reason for the pause.

"Hopefully, she recovers soon," Walt interjected.

Bill's eyes seemed to glaze over into an unblinking stare.

Heidi sensed his unease and changed the subject. "So, how'd you get into the furniture business?"

"Sorta stumbled into it when my brother asked me about a table that needed some repairs. I loved the work. Started with a company and later branched out on my own. All the furniture I work on these days is from European immigrants whose descendants want Joan and me to restore their antiques to their original glory. Come on inside. I have a lot of pieces to show off."

They obliged and followed Bill inside to a living room with a sofa, chair, and television. A cluttered kitchen occupied a room off to the side. Beyond the living room was an area filled with furniture neatly arranged in rows, with corridors barely wide enough for a person to pass through. A chain cordoned off the stairs. Hanging from it was a sign that read "private". Under the stairs was a half open cupboard. Rather than explaining anything about the furniture in the room, Bill told us about a little boy whose ghost lives there. Heidi thought of Harry Potter's cupboard under the stairs. The similarity between these locations made her doubt Tom's story. Then she recalled films about the Mafia and felt prickles well-up on her arms, but Buddy stood unflinching. It was time to get out of the house and back into the open air. She gave a customary nod to Walt to indicate she was ready to go. With thanks and handshakes, they departed, with Buddy happily trotting alongside.

∽

During one outing, Buddy was so excited he leapt energetically out of Heidi's open car window when she stepped a few feet away to locate a trailhead. She was glad she'd left Jack at home since he wasn't particularly bright and would likely have taken a perilous jump out the window. Jack would run away at home in pursuit of a squirrel, oblivious to oncoming traffic. Suffice to say, after several occurrences, he was never let out of the fenced yard again. Despite Jack's cognitive disabilities, Buddy had become his best friend. At home, they slept together in an unlocked crate. Jack's tendency to use the crate like a cat's litter box rather than asking to go outside didn't seem to trouble Buddy. He managed to stay dry. Heidi chose to clean it every day since she couldn't stop the negative behavior.

When Jack eventually passed, Buddy refused to enter their shared crate ever again without whimpering and pulling back. Cleaning it with scent-eradicating cleansers didn't change his mind, so Walt bought a new one. Without his companion, Buddy became more dependent on Heidi and barked incessantly whenever she needed to leave him home alone. On one occasion, she took him with her and tied him to a post outside a building where she could see him while she was getting her blood drawn. It wasn't a very good post and bent over, upsetting a woman passing by. Leaving him in the hot car, even with the windows cracked, wasn't an option either, as people tended to call the police whenever they saw a dog in a car. So, for his sake and hers, he had to stay home alone in the crate for all future appointments. If he'd been an official service dog with a corresponding vest, he could have come into public establishments. Even so, he had a good life.

⌒⊘

In his thirteenth-year, Buddy woke in the middle of the night. Heidi heard him utter a soft squeak, or was it a groan? It was hard to tell, being half awake under her quilts. Thud. The sound could only have been him rolling off the 3-inch-thick mattress onto the floor beside their bed. Peering over the edge into the abyss, she saw him sprawled out on the wooden floor with his legs spread out to the side of his body. The groan became an insistent whimper. At the same time, he appeared to be saying, no hurry, while looking up at Heidi with the sides of his mouth pulled back into a smile (everyone knows dogs don't smile). The moonlight reflected off his half-blind, milky eyes. Slithering out of bed, she stretched her hands toward the ceiling and cracked her back before attempting to lift him onto his feet. Once done, he strolled back onto the little bed, where he curled up again. On some nights, this routine would happen once, others twice. Yet, she never woke Walt to ask for help because his workday started at four in the morning. She never wanted to disrupt his sleep. Years before, when they had newborn babies, he'd always be half asleep with his hand draped over the baby in the basket next to their bed while she slept soundly, knowing they were in his capable care until it was time to nurse them.

But one night, the scene changed. Two blankets lay precariously in front of a church where Walt, Buddy, and Heidi were huddled together, hoping to avoid being discovered by the pastor. Life had taken a hard turn, not only for Buddy, but for his parents. Suddenly, a light flicked on behind Heidi, casting shadows through the cracks in the door of the alcove. Her hand brushed against something—it was a note from Walt. He'd gone to the car at the end of the lane, and they were to meet him there. Buddy, ever loyal, stood up beside her, no matter what the cost. Even if it meant watching Walt roll away. Buddy tried to drag his blanket along with his teeth, but it was too cumbersome and stumbled multiple times. The tension mounted.

Heidi collected both their blankets and her backpack. They had to escape before the person who had turned on the light discovered them. They had only intended to stay the night, yet now they fled, propelled by the urgency of their perceived situation. Although it was their choice to travel this way, seeking a new perspective, the reality was fraught with uncertainty.

A short walk away, Heidi saw their red jeep. The fumes floated out of the exhaust pipe. Walt's wheelchair waited by the door for her to mount on the back. She rubbed her eyes and yawned, but consoled herself as she always did. Life could be worse. The back latch stuck. Pulling and tugging repeatedly, she got it open. Buddy jumped inside and onto the pile of quilts on the backseat. Moving the wheelchair after it was folded required rocking it sideways and heaving it upward using all the strength in her back and arms.

The air felt thick. She glanced over her shoulder, half expecting someone to emerge from the shadows. A cold sweat formed on her brow. The seconds ticked by; the jeep's engine idled roughly. A faint rustling behind the nearby bushes heightened her senses. Her mind raced through potential threats. Was someone other than the clergyman watching them? Even if it was him, why would he remain concealed? Heidi fastened the straps on the wheelchair while her hands trembled. Calling out to Walt occurred to her. Except he wouldn't be able to help. An unexpected chill came over her, and her breath hitched. Was this just paranoia?

Then she broke free of the spell. This tale was only a dream, a lucid one, that Heidi manipulated as she woke. The wheelchair became a backpack. Having Walt disabled and the inevitable consequences wasn't really their life.

Yet, the lingering unease remained. Even as reality set in, she couldn't shake the feeling that something unpleasant was lurking out of sight, waiting. The dream was surely spurred by her anxieties about the upcoming sale of their house, along with the intended journey across the country to help Walt's relatives. They had waited several years to receive a contract. The current one was pending because the purchaser had fallen off a roof while working in the city. His family thought he might be bound to a wheelchair, and the 5-acre property required a substantial amount of maintenance. Heidi worried about them rather than herself and Walt. They could always put it back on the market. Their minds spun in many directions while praying the man healed, regardless of the outcome of the sale. After getting over the shock of the accident, the contract settled. Even if the new owner had to be in a wheelchair, he still wanted their home because the majority of the house was on one level. As time passed, he recovered full mobility, and the family cherished the property according to reports from the neighbors. They filled the property with graceful horses, stubborn tricolor goats, and a flock of fancy chickens. By day they worked; by night they frolicked in the pool and held parties with mariachi bands to celebrate their renewed life.

As for Buddy, he passed away before the family's final departure from the house. The vet said he had cancer in the membrane that surrounded his liver. The pain pills helped him eat for a few days, but then he'd stop. Every time Heidi switched to a different brand, the outcome remained the same. Within a month, he couldn't be left alone in the house to wander. Whenever he got off his bed, he'd stand up, but the hardwood floor hurt his hips and he'd go back to bed. One morning, Heidi went outside to pick some vegetables and returned to find him on the floor with his legs splayed. He couldn't get up and was whimpering. She was able to pull him onto his feet and return him to his bed. If he'd still weighed eighty as he had in his younger years, she wouldn't have been able to help him. Nothing improved as the month progressed.

The family decided Buddy's suffering should end. Keeping him going for their sake wasn't humane. Walt lifted him into the car, and they headed to the vet's office. In the exam room, Dr. Short brought in a blanket for Buddy to rest on the floor, and they all sat down next to him. He put his head in Heidi's lap and gazed up at her with his puppy eyes to say goodbye. Those eyes, the eyes she first gazed into thirteen years before. Those eyes had said and still said, *I'm yours forever. When you see a shadow out of the corner of your eye, it will be me.* The doctor cried along with them as she gave the injection. He gently slipped away into another world. Some say, 'he crossed the rainbow bridge.' Heidi never quite understood what that meant other than crossing over to animal heaven to wait for loved humans to appear. But his eyes told a different story.

A month after Buddy's death, a small package arrived with a custom-made ceramic vase. The outside had hair burnt onto the surface. The chemicals present in them during the firing process resulted in various bursts of color appearing randomly along the strands. In their new home, she planned to put it on a shelf with the bigger vase embedded with the remnants from Cody's tail. Heidi's favorite dog, her favorite horse. Both gone. Never again to have two better family friends.

"…Where in long evenings there are a million fireplace with logs forever burning, and one curls oneself up and blinks into the flames and nods and dreams, remembering the old brave days on earth and the love…"

—Eugene O'Neill. Born 1888, died 1953. Quote from *The Last Will & Testament of an Extremely Distinguished Dog.*

Dear Reader

I hope you enjoyed this collection. Please consider posting your honest review on websites such as Goodreads or Amazon or any other site that appeals to you. Your thoughts will encourage my future projects and help other readers become interested in my writing.

Thank you,

Elsa